The Face Behind the Mask

The Face
Behind
the Mask

John Minahan

W·W·Norton & Company
New York · London

233275

The text of this book is composed in Times Roman, with display type set in Trump Bold. Composition and manufacturing by The Haddon Craftsmen, Inc.

First Edition

Library of Congress Cataloging in Publication Data

Minahan, John.
The face behind the mask.

I. Title.
PS3563.I4616F3   1986   813'.54   85-7304

ISBN 0-393-02252-8

W. W. Norton & Company, Inc.
500 Fifth Avenue, New York, N. Y. 10110
W. W. Norton & Company Ltd.
37 Great Russell Street, London WC1B 3NU

1 2 3 4 5 6 7 8 9 0

Acknowledgments

I want to express my appreciation for the technical advice of John Gaulrapp, Brendan Tumulty, Happy Goday, Robert M. Cavallo, and the Police Department of the City of New York.

J. M.

To John Gaulrapp,
the finest detective I've ever known.

This is what we most abhor:
The face behind the mask.
        HERMAN MELVILLE

The Face Behind the Mask

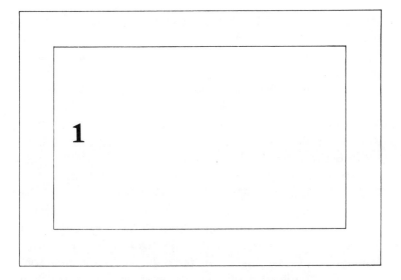

1

THAT DAY IS FROZEN in my mind: Tuesday, October 11, 1983. We're in the squadroom, early afternoon, Lieutenant Barnett sends Brendan Thomas and me to interview a complainant, Miss Dawn Harkness, 240 East Seventy-third Street, apartment 23-B. We get up there about 2:15, Harkness turns out to be a sixteen-year-old kid, looks older, well endowed, dark hair and eyes, extremely attractive. Lives with her mother, an executive secretary; she's been called, she's on her way home now. Dawn's pale, she's crying, hands are shaking, wrists are red. We sit in the living room, try to calm her down, speak quietly, ask her to start at the beginning. Tells us she's a junior at Cathedral High School, 350 East Fifty-sixth. Had no afternoon classes today, so she gets home about 12:30. After taking a shower, she begins pressing her uniform to go to McDonald's, Third and Seventy-sixth, where she works part time. Phone rings and a male voice asks if Miss E. Harkness is home. No, who's calling, please? Says his name is Jim Burns from Manhattan Mutual Insurance Company. Says Miss E.

Harkness of 240 East Seventy-third filled out a policy application, mailed it in, but forgot to sign it. He's in the immediate area and would like to drop it off. Dawn tells him there's no *Miss* E. Harkness here, but her mother's first name is Elizabeth. He asks to speak with her. Sorry, she's at work, won't be home until around six. He says he's visiting another client just around the corner, he'd like to drop it off, she can mail it back. Sounds very businesslike. Dawn says okay, but to hurry because she has to leave soon.

Five minutes later, doorman rings on the intercom: Mr. Burns of Manhattan Mutual Insurance Company is in the lobby, says he's expected. Yes, please send him up. Minute later, doorbell rings. She looks through the peephole, sees a young man in a business suit. Asks who he is. Jim Burns, Manhattan Mutual. She opens the door, keeps the chain on. He's holding a large manila envelope; explains there are two signatures required, he'll have to show her, only take a few seconds. Guy is clean-cut all the way, handsome, executive type, she feels silly hiding behind the door like this. She slips the chain, he walks in, opens the envelope, takes out some papers, places them on the hall table.

Now he kicks the door shut, pulls a gun. "Not a *word*. Not one word or I'll have to kill you. I'm a junkie, I need cash. Give me all the cash and jewelry in the house. Fast. Move it."

Dawn opens a desk drawer, gives him $102 in cash, says that's all the money in the house. He tells her to go in her mother's bedroom, get all the jewelry. They go in, she gives him everything she can find, which isn't much, explains that her mother always wears her best jewelry to work.

He points the gun at her face. "Take all your clothes off and you won't get hurt." She begins to cry and begs him not to touch her. He cocks the gun. "You have exactly ten seconds. Strip or die, it's up to you." She removes her bathrobe and undergarments, stands in front of him nude, crying, head down. "Lie on the bed and spread your legs." She pleads, crys, but does as she's told. He uncocks the gun, places it on the floor, removes his clothes quickly, picks up the gun. Asks how old she is. She says she's fifteen, a sophomore in high school. "You're a God damn liar! You're at least eighteen!" She turns, puts her face in the pillow, starts crying again. "Stop that shit and look at me! Keep looking at me!" Grabs her feet, pulls her toward him until her legs are over the end of the bed. Now he stands over her, begins stroking his penis. She turns away. "You better look, bitch! You don't know how lucky you are to be fifteen!" Finally ejaculates over her breasts and stomach. "Y'know, bitch, you got a beautiful body. Maybe I'll stop back on your sixteenth birthday."

He takes out a penknife, cuts the long telephone wire at both ends, then cuts it in half. Tells her to lie on her stomach, ties her hands behind her back, ties her feet, gags her with a scarf. Gets dressed quickly, works on his necktie carefully in front of a mirror. Holsters the gun, puts the papers back in the manila envelope, leaves quickly. Whole thing takes less than fifteen minutes.

Takes Dawn almost an hour to get free. She's exhausted, but the first thing she does is take a shower to "get that animal's filth off me." Gets dressed, goes to her neighbor's apartment, calls the police, then her mother, who should be home momentarily.

Brendan glances at me, flips a page in his notebook, touches his trim mustache. He's trying to remain calm, but I can see it in his eyes. Old buddy of mine, best partner I ever had, forty-four, six-foot-four, 220, hails from Wicklow, Ireland. Speaks with a brogue on certain words. "Okay, Dawn. If you feel up to it, we'd like to ask you a few questions. Or would you rather wait till your mother gets here?"

"I'd rather answer them now."

"How old are you?" he asks.

"Sixteen. I'll be seventeen in January."

"Why'd you tell him fifteen?"

She takes a swipe at her dark hair. "I don't know, it was the first thing that came to mind. If he thought I was a juvenile he might back off. That really made him mad. He kept talking about that."

"And he told you he was a junkie?" I ask.

"Yeah. That he had to steal to support his habit."

"Did you notice any tracks or needle marks on his arms?"

She thinks about it. "No. No, none at all. And he made me stare at him. He looked too healthy to be on drugs."

"Could you describe him to us?" Brendan asks.

"Yes. I think he was about six feet tall and had brown hair, light brown. He looked like he just had a haircut. He had blue eyes. Very, very blue, and was clean-shaven. He wore a dark gray, pin-stripe suit with a white button-down shirt and a maroon tie."

"How about his weight?" I ask.

"I'm not good on men's weights, but I'd guess—maybe one eighty-five, somewhere in there. He looked like he was in good shape."

"Age?" Brendan asks.

"I'd say mid-thirties."

"Any scars or marks?"

"No, nothing. He was—I don't know if this helps, but he was unusually good-looking, y'know?"

I sit forward, turn the page in my notebook. "Good-looking enough to be a model?"

She hesitates. "No. No, I don't think so. He just didn't seem to be that type guy, y'know?"

"Now, the gun," Brendan says. "Could you describe that?"

"Yeah. It was small and black with a brown handle. I could see the bullets when he pointed it at my face."

"Which hand did he hold it in?"

"His right hand, but the holster was on his left side. I remember that, a small black holster on the left side of his belt."

Mrs. Harkness arrives about then, frantic, attractive lady in her early forties, fashionably dressed. She rushes to Dawn, hugs her, kisses her, begins to cry, gets Dawn started again. We stand back until they're finished, then introduce ourselves. Mrs. Harkness goes to the kitchen, pours herself a stiff drink, comes back and sits with us in the living room.

Brendan and I explain basically what happened. Tell Mrs. Harkness that, bad as it was, it could've been much worse, that whole routine, which happens to be true in this case. We offer to take Dawn to the hospital for a general checkup, but she refuses politely. Her wrists and ankles are sore, but that's about it. Question Mrs. Harkness about the insurance policy application with Manhattan Mutual. Never filled one out. Ask if her telephone number is listed. Yes, under E. Harkness. Seems our friend is selecting names without the gender listed. If he tries enough numbers, he's got to get lucky.

Finally we ask Mrs. Harkness if we could take them downtown, so Dawn could view photos of sex offenders and rapists, providing she feels up to it. "I'm up to it," Dawn snaps. "Let's go." While they get ready, Brendan calls the office, fills in Lieutenant Barnett, asks him to order a check on similar MOs. In the lobby we speak to the doorman who admitted Mr. Burns. Says he'd be able to identify him if necessary.

At 3:10 we drive Dawn and her mother to the Bureau of Criminal Identification, headquarters, 1 Police Plaza. Two hours of viewing mug shots. Negative results.

Return them to the apartment about 5:30. Dust any areas Dawn thinks the man may have touched. Explain we'll have to take their own fingerprints, plus those of any friends who visit frequently, for purposes of elimination. Mrs. Harkness agrees to assemble these people the following evening. Although it's highly unlikely that Mr. Burns is actually a representative of Manhattan Mutual, we'll want Dawn to look through the company's personnel photos, particularly those of recently dismissed employees. An appointment will be made with the police artist to draw a sketch based on Dawn's description. In the event that a suspect is apprehended, we'll want Dawn to view a lineup. We're guaranteed full cooperation. Schedule: Tomorrow afternoon we'll pick Dawn up at the apartment after school, take her to the insurance company, then to the artist at headquarters, then return to the apartment to fingerprint Dawn, her mother, and all frequent visitors.

Driving back to the Nineteenth Precinct, Brendan and I talk about the case. Dawn seems to be a nice kid, bright, pretty, eager to cooperate. Hate to think of what she went through. It's bad enough when adult women are involved, but when a kid like this is victimized, even if she isn't physically hurt (many of them are), it gives you a sick feeling in your gut. More than that, much more, if I'm honest: It makes me angry, it gets to me on a personal level, which is dangerous. Not too long ago, most cases like this wouldn't even be reported; too embarrassing, too much of a hassle for the victim, not nearly enough consideration for her. It's a different world today, at least in this city, women are fed up with this crap, most of them report attacks fast, they follow up with a vengeance, they're not satisfied until they get a conviction and the sicko's put in a cage for the maximum allowable or close to it. Unfortunately, few of them actually get that satisfaction. Convictions are still extremely difficult in most rape cases. Major stumbling block is corroborative evidence. But we've come a long way from the old days.

Arrive back at the precinct about 5:55, Nineteenth Precinct, 153 East Sixty-seventh, between Lex and Third. Rush hour is well underway, street is jammed with taxis, cars, vans, trucks, sidewalks are crowded, everybody's in the usual hurry. Cool autumn afternoon, sun's slanting through the canyon to color our old building dirty shades of gray and gold. Six or eight men, uniformed cops and detectives, are standing on the old stone steps, talking, laughing, smoking, most of them look very young to me. Seem to look younger every year, but they're not. Twelve of my twenty-eight years in the department have been spent in this precinct, relatively happy years for the most part, and I realize only too well that I'll probably hang it up here, sooner or later. Fine with me, as long as it's later. I turned fifty this year, the Big Five-O, July 30, 1983. Hard to believe. Don't feel fifty, don't feel anywhere near it. Don't look it, either, compared to most. But that's my opinion. Must say, I had mixed feelings when Catherine and I celebrated with the family. Now, just over two months later, it's beginning to sink in. Fifty. Christ. But, I figure, so what? In my judgment, age has nothing to do with numbers, it all depends on the individual.

It's all relative, as they say. Take our precinct, for example, and compare it to some of the relatively newer ones around town. No contest. Constructed in 1887 (second oldest in the city), this one's got more class than any of them, it's now a Designated New York City Landmark. Exterior can't be altered without permission from the Landmarks Preservation Commission. Five stories of graceful but solid architecture, built to last, built by men with genuine pride in their work, built with materials you won't find in any "modern" structure anywhere in the city. Take a long hard look at this place when you get a chance, walk in through the tall stone archway, tell the desk sergeant you heard about it and want to see for yourself. Probably get a smile out of him. Fact is, many of the cops who work here don't share my feelings about the place. Why? No creature comforts. No central heating or air conditioning, no elevators, no modern bathrooms or locker rooms or any of the fancy furniture and fixtures that are now more or less standard in the newer precincts. Some of the younger cops around here, the television generation, they hear me talk about this place, they give me this look. Like I should be a Designated New York City Landmark myself. Fine with me. I'm talking ninety-six years of NYPD history here, not *Return of the Jedi.*

I mean, get this: In 1887, and for ten years later, this pre-

cinct had *gaslights.* Outside, horses clomped by on the cob-
blestone street until almost the turn of the century. In 1887,
Stephen Grover Cleveland was President; Queen Victoria
celebrated her Golden Jubilee; and Sir Arthur Conan
Doyle's first Sherlock Holmes story, *A Study in Scarlet,* was
published. In 1887, Detroit won the National League pennant under manager W.H. Watkins (the American League
didn't even exist until 1901); Big Sam Thompson of Detroit
won the batting championship with a .372 average; and Bill
O'Brien of Washington won the home run crown with a re-
sounding nineteen. Pitching? Ready for this? In 1887, John
Clarkson of Chicago won 38, lost 21, struck out 237, and
completed 56 games out of 60. That was in a 124-game season, mind you. Didn't get elected to the Hall of Fame until
1963, but you can't win 'em all.

Back to the present. Brendan and I go inside, climb the old
reinforced stairway to the second floor. Squadroom is off to
the left, back of the building, breathtaking view of the alley.
Door's never locked. Always gives me a comfortable feeling
to walk in here. Big rectangular room, high ceiling, fluorescent
lights, thick blue-painted walls, green linoleum floor. Tall windows with outside bars. Steam radiators. Lieutenant's office to
the far right, two sergeants' offices to the far left. My desk (not
exclusively mine, used by detectives on the two other shifts)
is in the corner to the right, just outside the lieutenant's office.
Like all the other desks in the room, mine is a small steel job,
dark-green body, light-green top. Typewriter is a vintage
Royal manual. Wall behind to my left holds the most recent
"wanted" posters and a big calendar. Wall to my right near
the windows holds an electric clock, then a series of nineteen
small wooden plaques with the hand-painted names of every
detective in the squad, arranged in the chain-of-command.
Brendan's desk is on the other side of the room. Focal point
of the joint is located to the right of the lieutenant's office, our
department-famous old-fashioned "holding area" that actu-

ally dates from 1887: A small square cage, out in the open, with four walls of crisscrossed steel bars extending all the way to the ceiling, maybe fifteen feet high. Nothing inside but the floor. Suspects sit on it while we do our paperwork. Nobody in there now, but, on average, we'll have at least four suspects in there during every twenty-four hour period, 365 days a year. Figure it out. In ninety-six years, that multiplies to more than 140,000 suspects cooling it in the cage. Quite a few infamous names, too. Story goes, in the Roaring 'Twenties, that cage held the likes of Pretty Boy Floyd and Baby Face Nelson. To name just a few. No other precinct in the city can make that claim. History? Tell me about it.

Brendan and I have a quick conference with Lieutenant Barnett. He's been around a while like us, late forties, short, lean, hair more white than gray. Tells us detectives Telfian and Thalheimer are now in an apartment at 515 East Eighty-fifth, interviewing a complainant on an attempted rape and robbery. Telfian called in about twenty minutes ago.

"Sounds like the same gent," Barnett says. "Height, weight, the blue-blue eyes, even the insurance farce. They'll be back with the report shortly. Meantime, I've contacted Chief Vadney's office and the Manhattan Borough office regarding recent similar MOs. I'm waiting for their reports."

About 6:20 Rick Telfian and Gene Thalheimer get back from their interview. We all sit down in Barnett's office. Rick, he's always smiling, never takes anything too seriously: "Should've been with us on this one, Brendan. Nice young Irish gal, fresh from the old sod."

"Just read the report," Barnett says tiredly.

Telfian smiles, sits back, lights up a cigar. Tough little Armenian, short, muscular, hell of a semipro shortstop. Flips open his notebook. "At about three forty-five P.M., the live-in maid at the apartment, Miss Sheila McKenzie, receives a call from a Mr. Burns of Manhattan Mutual Insurance Company. Wants to talk to Miss B. Loudenville about an insurance application to be signed, says he's in the area. Maid explains that it's *Mrs.* Loudenville, that she's recovering from pneumonia and confined to bed. Mr. Burns says he's sorry to hear that, but if he could just drop it off, she could endorse it and mail it back at her convenience. Miss McKenzie gives him the okay. Minutes later he's inside the apartment, pistol drawn: 'Scream and you're both dead.' McKenzie explains that Mrs. Loudenville is an old lady, very ill, sleeping. Burns tells her to go in the old lady's room, bring out her jewel box, then give him all the cash that's in the house. If she tries anything, they're both dead. She gives him the jewel box and about two hundred in cash. Now Burns grabs her around the neck, rips off her blouse and bra. Swings her around, sticks the gun in her chest and tells her to get down on her knees. Then he takes Oscar out and orders her to go to work. You'll love this, Brendan."

"Rick," Barnett snaps. "Just read the report, will ya!"

Telfian smiles, puffs the cigar. "Now, Sheila McKenzie, who happens to be twenty-three years old and has physical characteristics that allow her to do heavy housework, she looks up at Mr. Burns, she says—and this is a direct quote, you can ask Gene here—she says, 'Ya dirty, filthy pig, ya! I'll have ya know, I'm a devout Roman Catholic, I've never in me life done such a dirty, filthy, sacrilegious deed, and I never will!' With that, she throws a fast, vicious uppercut to his testicles. The dude levitates with an earsplitting roar and punches her in the face, knocking her across the room. She screams bloody murder. By now, old Mrs. Loudenville is out of her bedroom, screaming and shouting, and Mr. Burns makes a hasty exit, grabbing his manila envelope with one hand and trying to rearrange his badly brused three-piece set with the other. Miss McKenzie calls the police. A radio car responds, but the subject's long gone. The doorman and a resident saw him leave, but were unaware that anything happened. They think they can ID him and will be available if necessary. Miss McKenzie refuses medical attention, she says —again, this is a direct quote, you can ask Gene—she says, 'That dirty little pig needs it more than me.' According to her, Burns didn't touch anything that could be dusted, so we didn't bother. McKenzie will look at mug shots in the morning and assist in any way she can."

About 6:45, we're typing up our reports when Mat Murphy calls from Chief Vadney's office, wants to speak with Barnett, who's already gone home. Mat and me go back a long way, so he tells me what's going down. Our man Burns has been very active during the past three weeks, pole-vaulting all over town. One case is of particular importance, triggers a whole series of top-level events within the department. On Friday, September 23, in the Twentieth Precinct jurisdiction, a young bride-to-be was raped and sodomized. Not just *any* young bride-to-be. Name is Belinda Ballanger, twenty-two. Her father is Henry Ballanger, senior partner in a major Manhattan law firm—and a close personal friend of Police Commissioner Reilly. Seems they were fraternity brothers at Columbia, same class. Needless to say, there's heavy emotional involvement here, case gets top priority, no publicity of any kind whatsoever. Commissioner's on Chief Vadney's back from the opening bell, he wants action, he wants all stops pulled. Vadney immediately forms a special assignment team of thirty-five handpicked detectives from all five boroughs. Lieutenant Marty Shugrue of the Twentieth Precinct is team supervisor, reports directly to Vadney, who reports directly to Commissioner Reilly.

Mat goes on to give me some intriguing tidbits. Over the past eighteen days, there have been a total of seven rapes in the Bronx with almost identical MOs, except that in the Bronx, for some reason, no robberies were involved. In addition to the special assignment team, all those cases are being investigated by the Bronx Sex Crime Unit. Mat says, "Wait a minute," puts me on hold. When he doesn't get back to me for several minutes, I cradle the receiver in my neck and shoulder, go back to typing my report.

Click. "John, just talked to Vadney. He's already scheduled a meeting in his office tomorrow morning: Marty Shugrue with two of his men, Dave Pearson of the Bronx Unit with two of his men; and he wants you and Brendan, Telfian and Thalheimer. Ten o'clock sharp. I suggest you guys get your reports typed up nice and clean."

"Blue Duo-Tang presentation folders?"

"Believe it. Clean copies, three-hole punched."

"Sincere suits?"

"Best *dark* sincere suits."

On the train home to Bellmore, L.I., that evening, I concentrate on the sports pages of the *Post.* World Series starts tonight, October 11, Philadelphia at Baltimore, 8:30 EST. I plan to watch. These days, only one player grabs my attention, Pete Rose of the Phillies. I identify with this guy. Here he is, forty-two years old, "Charlie Hustle," twenty-one seasons in the bigs, 3,990 major league hits, only 201 away from Ty Cobb's all-time record of 4,191, one of the last theoretically "unbreakable" records in baseball history. Rose is healthy, he's psyched up, as usual, but don't forget he was benched toward the end of the season, first time in his career, because he wasn't hitting (finished the season with a .245 average, his all-time low). During the crunch drive for the pennant, Phillies' manager Paul Owens replaced Rose with rookie first baseman Len Matuszek, but he didn't bring the kid up soon enough to be eligible for the playoffs or World Series. So now he's got to play Rose, like it or not, and I'm pulling for Pete to come on strong, to show everybody he's still got it. No matter what happens, I have a gut feeling Rose won't be back with the Phils next season. Reason? They probably won't play him regularly, they're on a youth kick now, and Pete's contract expires at the end of postseason play this year. Obviously, Rose has to play regularly (at least 130–140 games) for another season and a half to get a realistic shot at Cobb's record, which has remained unchallenged since 1928. I think Pete's got two good seasons left in him, maybe three. Cobb didn't hang it up until he'd played twenty-four years, but he started in the majors at age nineteen, three years younger than Rose, and he retired at forty-two. Still, I think Rose will catch him. I really do. He's that kind of competitor. As I said before, I don't think age has anything to do with numbers, I think it all depends on the individual. Rose looks and plays like he's thirty-five.

It's twilight when the train enters Nassau County and rattles through the little towns of Valley Stream, Lynbrook, Rockville Centre, and Baldwin. I light up a cigar, look out the window, and think about the Series. Sportswriters have dubbed the 1983 Phillies "The Wheeze Kids" because Rose, Joe Morgan, and Tony Perez are all over forty, and the team's average age is thirty-five. If you're a real baseball fan, you know that's a comparison to the famous 1950 Phillies, "The Whiz Kids," who won the pennant in a breeze, then lost four straight to the Yankees in the World Series. Thirty-three years ago, but I remember those kids vividly. Guys like Richie Ashburn, Dick Sisler, Eddie Waitkus, Puddin' Head Jones, Del Ennis, Granny Hamner, Mike Goliat, Andy Seminick, Robin Roberts. Of course, they were playing one of the great Yankee lineups of the decade: Johnny Mize, Hank Bauer, Yogi Berra, Joe DiMaggio, Jerry Coleman, Gene Woodling, Phil Rizzuto, Bobby Brown, Allie Reynolds, Vic Raschi, Whitey Ford. Hard to believe, but in 1950 Pete Rose was nine years old, playing sandlot ball in Cincinnati.

Arrive in Bellmore at 8:10, just about on schedule. Although I usually walk home on pleasant evenings like this, tonight Catherine's waiting for me in the car (I called her from Penn Station), because I don't want to miss the opening ceremonies for the game. Our son John is in the back, wearing his Yankee cap, he's really looking forward to tonight, gets to stay up late. John's seven, our only child. He's not John Jr., he's John Christopher; I'm John Phillip. The Yankees are our favorite team and I happen to be partial to Graig Nettles, I think he's the classiest third baseman in baseball today. But the Yankees didn't even make the playoffs this year, of course, they finished third. My opinion, they were lucky to finish that high.

Tell you what, John's getting to be quite a ballplayer himself. This past summer he played shortstop for the Pirates in the CYO League out here (ages six and seven), and he had one hell of a good season. Hate to brag about the kid, *but.* Right? But I can't help mentioning just one statistic. This season (April through June), in sixteen games, John had twenty-two hits in twenty-three official trips to the plate. Sounds unbelievable, I know, but it's a fact. So his official CYO average this year was .956, tops in the league, of course. Only one home run, but keep in mind he's a shortstop. Kid's a slap hitter like I was, a legger, consistent line-drive type guy. Gets on base, lets the bigger kids drive him home. Not that he's small for his age: Four-foot-two, fifty-six pounds, just about average. Lean and wiry, ideal for a shortstop. Goes to his left and right pretty good, covers a lot of ground.

"Who you for tonight?" I ask him.

"Orioles. I like Cal Ripken."

"Ripken? What about Pete *Rose?*"

"Yeah, but he's not a shortstop."

"Well, how about DeJesus?"

"Oh, Dad, come on. No comparison.

"One of the best shortstops in the league."

"No way. Good field, no hit."

"You finish your homework?"

"You kidding? *Hours* ago!"

We pull in the driveway and park. Almost 8:15. The lighted windows of our living room throw yellow rectangles across the lawn. Modest two-story house, natural cedar shingles, four bedrooms, two baths, quiet residential neighborhood. As we walk to the front door, the wind blows clusters of leaves down across the grass and there's a strong smell of rain.

Eileen is in the family room in back watching the pregame ceremonies. She's Catherine's younger sister who's living with us, an executive secretary at Mobil Oil in Manhattan. Bright, attractive lady, we get along very well.

"It's raining in Baltimore," she tells us.

"Oh, no," Catherine says.

"Just a light shower so far."

Catherine goes in the kitchen, John grabs a Pepsi and sits on the floor near the TV, Eileen stays put. I take off my coat and tie, loosen my collar, pour myself a very dry Beefeater martini on the rocks. Now I lean against the counter, watch Catherine check her homemade lasagna, one of my favorites. Her light brunette hair is worn relatively short these days, makes her look younger. She glances up at me, bright blue eyes smiling behind her glasses, then we both look in at John, sitting cross-legged in front of the set, Yankee cap still on, Pepsi in hand.

Less than nine years ago, Catherine and I had just about resigned ourselves to the fact that we probably wouldn't be able to have children. We wanted a family very much, but we just couldn't seem to get the right chemistry together. We even considered adoption. After waiting eighteen years and almost giving up hope, when John was born, December 14, 1975, it seemed like a miracle to us. Still does. Still find myself staring at him and shaking my head.

All kinds of people keep telling me that when you actually reach the age of fifty, the fact doesn't sink in at first, there's a delayed reaction, then it hits you, and you start reflecting back on your life. I don't really believe it. Still, I think those people planted a seed in my mind, because lately I've caught myself looking back more than usual, doing some mental arithmetic, adding up the major things. Difficult to explain, because it's not really a conscious process. Usually happens when I'm happy like tonight. I'm sipping the martini, looking at John, and I'm thinking back on my life. Can't seem to help it. I'm not a very religious man, but whenever I reflect on things, I thank God in my own private way. I consider myself a very fortunate man. I have a wife I love, a good marriage that's lasted twenty-six years now, a healthy son I love more than my life, and a job I've enjoyed—most of the time—for twenty-eight years. That's not bad. Not bad for a kid from the lower East Side who never even had an opportunity to go to college.

I'm no angel, never have been, but the plain, simple truth is—corny as it may seem today—Catherine and I decided from the very beginning that no matter what happened, we'd try to be honest in our lives. And we've kept to that. Sounds easy, but it's not. If there's any single key to the happiness we've had in our lives, I think that's probably it.

In my line of work, you tend to see the worst elements in our society. And I mean the whole range from murderers, dope dealers, rapists, arsonists, child molesters, and common thieves, all the way to so-called white-collar criminals, educated people with all the advantages, who seem to have no morals whatsoever. Dealing with these people on a day-to-day basis, year after year, gets to a lot of cops, it's often seriously depressing. That's why so many of us try to develop a good sense of humor. In my judgment, you can't really work effectively without it. If you go in as an idealist, and you don't roll with the punches, chances are, you'll come out broken.

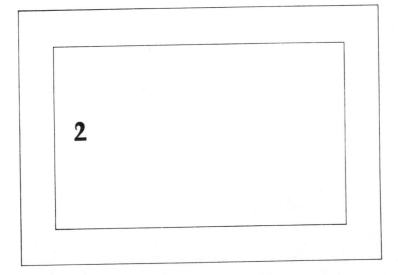

2

FIRST THING THAT HITS YOU about Chief Vadney's newly decorated office is his desk. Not a desk in the conventional sense, mind you, this thing is actually—well, what it is, it's a conference table. Sort of a scaled-down version of a Fortune 500 corporate board of directors table. Twelve feet by six feet. Highly polished teakwood. Chrome-plated legs. Twelve modern executive armchairs, real black leather tufted cushions, chrome-plated frames, wheels. Each place setting has a single yellow legal pad and a single yellow pencil alongside, sharpened to a lethal point. Chief's silver Sony TCM-600 Cassette-Corder occupies the precise center of the table, unobtrusively recording every sound on a Maxell UD-60 cassette, destined to take its place among the more than 500 other Maxell tapes, all carefully labeled and dated, in one of the twenty-six steel-blue filing cabinets that surround his large corner office. Chief sits at the end next to his new teakwood commode that holds his telephone console, his telephone recording equipment (legal), his telephone squawk box, and three 8"-✕-10" aluminum-framed, white-matted, black-and-white, head-and-shoulder photos of (left to right) Mayor Koch, Commissioner Reilly, and Wife Samantha. Solid chain of command.

It's ten o'clock sharp now and a total of ten detectives sit at the table, five to a side, in sincere suits of various subdued shades. Not a single ashtray in sight. Not a single cup of coffee, not even a glass of water. This is the new, improved, ultramodern, image-conscious 1983 NYPD Chief of Detectives' Desk. Purchased—ready for this?—purchased *personally* out of his own pocket last month (two-year installment plan) by a pissed-off Chief Vadney after a total of exactly twenty-seven official requests for same to Commissioner Reilly over a period of exactly twenty-seven consecutive months, dating roughly from the successful conclusion of the now-legendary Hotel Champs-Elysées heist, dubbed by the press as "The Great Hotel Robbery," specifically closed sometime in June 1981, can't remember the exact date. Commissioner kept turning him down on the grounds that it wasn't cost efficient. Chief finally called him a name. Called him a "cheap civilian tinhorn." Commissioner called him one back. Called him a "pathetic posturing punk." Anyhow, that's how he got the desk.

Chief's sky-blue Duke Wayne eyes glance first at his Omega Astronaut Moon Watch, then narrow to dark slits as he looks us over. Arches his left eyebrow. Purses his lips slowly, nods at Lieutenant Pearson of the Bronx Sex Crime Unit. "Dave, you lead it off, huh?"

Now, Dave Pearson, I've known him for ten years and I always respected him as one of the real class guys in the department. Dave's over fifty now, but still lean and wiry, high forehead, thinning hair, deeply lined face. Looks you straight in the eye, speaks softly but with authority, has a nice dry sense of humor. You look at this guy, you listen to him, you think, this is the type guy who would've made it big in public relations. Call it charisma, I don't know. If he'd gone into public relations as a young man, he'd be president of his own firm by now. We're lucky to have him.

Dave opens his folder, clears his throat. "Our first case was on Wednesday, September fourteenth, around two in the afternoon. A Miss Barbara Altman, white/forty-five, residing in the Riverdale section of the Bronx, was the first victim. She lives with a girl friend who was out at the time. Both work for the New York Telephone Company. I'm sure you're all familiar with the MO—telephone call, Mr. Burns of Manhattan Mutual Insurance, policy application to be signed. Anyway, she lets him in, he pulls a small black revolver from a belt holster, left side. He forced her to have oral sex, then raped her. Throughout the ordeal, Miss Altman studied the man's face and tried to keep a conversation going. She was determined to learn as much about him as possible. In our judgment, Altman will make an excellent witness and will cooperate all the way. The other six cases were basically the same with slight variations. In two cases, after oral sex, he Greeked 'em. Really hurt one girl, she had to be hospitalized. The guy must be hung like a mule."

Silence around the table.

"Dave," Chief says. "Without the personal opinion, huh?"

"Yes, sir. In all cases, the subject cut the telephone cords, tied and gagged 'em. He then wiped everything clean with a handkerchief. Apparently he takes his time doing this, very meticulous about it. One significant difference in his appearance, in the last two cases he wore a shoulder holster. Four of the victims refused to view photos; I don't know why they even bothered to report it. We've taken three of the victims to the police artist and now we have a composite sketch."

Pearson opens another folder, takes out a bunch of $8'' \times 10''$ black-and-white glossy photos of the sketch, passes them around. I take one look, I damn near laugh out loud. Subject happens to bear a distinct resemblance to the chief. Much younger, of course, at least fifteen years younger, but he's got the same Duke Wayne type weather-beaten features, macho-handsome. I exchange a glance with Brendan; he's picked up on it too. We both look at the chief. He's studying the sketch with a peculiar expression, brows knitted, two fingers to his nostrils like he's smelled something unpleasant.

"That's the consensus opinion of all three women," Pearson continues. "After nailing down the composite sketch, we took all three to BCI, total of three hours of viewing mug shots. Came up empty. We also took them to Manhattan Mutual where they viewed every duplicate ID photo of all employees, past and present. Struck out there too. We even toyed with the idea this guy might be enforcement—Correction, Housing, Transit, NYPD, even a Fed. So we took two of our better witnesses and went through the Identification Section of each job. They viewed every photo of every man with a description that was in any way similar to our subject. Zero. Next we checked the files of all officers fired or retired in the past couple of years. Zero. Chief Vadney, my recommendation would be to distribute this sketch to the news media at a formal press conference. Publication of the sketch may spook the guy, but then again it might stop him."

Silence. Chief leafs through his copy of Pearson's report. "All attacks were in the daytime, that correct?"

"Yes, sir. Mostly early afternoon. And none on weekends."

Chief nods. "Marty, give these guys from the Nineteenth a fast update on the Ballanger case."

Marty Shugrue, we've known Marty and his wife Marianne for years. Outstanding detective. Nice family, two girls, two boys. Originally from Providence, Rhode Island, graduated from Providence College in 1962. He's only forty-three now, tall, muscular, deep-set brown eyes, dark hair starting to recede on both sides of a prominent widow's peak. Spent six years as a carrier-based U.S. Navy pilot, now he's a Commander in the Reserve, still loves to fly. Thing about this guy, he's like a corporate executive but with a certain earthy quality.

First-class intelligence combined with the instincts of a street fighter. Worked his butt up the hard way, same as us. Loves to get out on the street with his men, kick ass, get his mitts dirty. Marianne and him, they got this beat-up old piano in their basement playroom, he knocks back a few drinks, starts banging away on that thing, singing with the crowd, forget it. This guy gets his chunk out of life.

Now he looks at us as he speaks, doesn't refer to his report at all. "The victim in my case is Miss Belinda Ballanger, twenty-two, of One-six-seven Riverside Drive, only daughter of Henry Ballanger, the well-known attorney, I'm sure you've heard of him. Same MO as the others. Friday, September twenty-third, she gets a call from Mr. Burns, Manhattan Mutual. Application for a policy was filled out by her roommate, Miss M. Levitt, but she didn't sign it. Wants to speak to her. Not home. Wants to drop it off. Miss Ballanger feels it's legit. Burns gets inside, pulls the gun—shoulder holster this time—sticks it to her head, says he'll kill her if she makes a sound."

"What time of day again?" Chief asks.

"Around one-thirty in the afternoon. He tells her to take her clothes off and get on the bed. She pleads with him, says she's a virgin, she's just become engaged. He starts with her, she puts up a struggle. He rips her clothes off, ties her up, gags her with her bra. First he sodomizes her, then he rapes her, turns into a real animal, makes a total mess of the kid. I don't take many things personally on this job, but I hope I get to meet this guy and he chooses to go the hard way. Miss Ballanger was taken to Roosevelt Hospital and had to be sedated. I spoke with her for a few minutes at the hospital. Dr. Thomas J. Rice, the attending physician, confirmed that she had in fact been a virgin, that she had been raped and suffered damage to the cervix, that she had been sodomized and sustained damage to the anal sphincter. Miss Ballanger is recovering at home now, under the care of a physician, and is apparently experiencing severe posttraumatic psychological symptoms. I tried to contact her at home several times and was informed that she wasn't really well enough to talk about it. Then I got a message from the Commissioner's office telling me to back off for a while. Anyway, the subject got away with a considerable amount of cash and jewelry, still undetermined, including the three-carat diamond engagement ring. That's about it."

"Thanks, Marty," Chief says quietly. "Sit tight now, don't get any ideas about head-huntin' on your own. Things aren't done that way any more."

Make a long story short, I give our report on the Harkness case, Gene Thalheimer reports on the McKenzie/Loudenville case. We all exchange copies of our typewritten reports. Before the meeting breaks up at 11:15, Chief calls Lieutenant Barnett, assigns me, Brendan, Telfian and Thalheimer to the special assignment team, full-time, effective immediately. On all ten cases to date, he wants detailed descriptions of the stolen property (with photographs if possible), he wants us to hit the pawnshops, all known fences, all regular informants, to kick ass if we have to, and to get the word out through the Diamond District about that three-carat ring: Anybody who touches that rock without dropping a dime to us is in deep shit. Also assigns a policewoman from the Manhattan Sex Crime Unit to interview reluctant witnesses, see if she can psych them into coming forward or at least get them to comment on the sketch. Finally, the chief approves Pearson's recommendation to release copies of the sketch to the news media at a formal press conference. Calls in Jerry Grady of Press Relations, tells him to set it up for 4:30 this afternoon, headquarters auditorium. Plenty of time to make the 6:00 and 11:00 local TV news shows; more than adequate time for the morning newspapers to give it priority space. Meeting dismissed.

Major breaks that afternoon: Commissioner Reilly convinces Henry Ballanger to allow his daughter to be interviewed by the top female detective in the Manhattan Sex

Crime Unit, girl by the name of Jessica Taylor. Interview will take place at Miss Ballanger's apartment, 167 Riverside, at 2:30. Meantime, Telfian and Thalheimer show the sketch to Sluggin' Sheila McKenzie, she makes a positive ID. Brendan and I get a positive ID on the sketch from Dawn Harkness.

After fingerprinting Mrs. Harkness, Dawn, and eight friends who are frequent visitors, Brendan and me are driving down to the Latent Fingerprint Section at headquarters, listening to the police radio, when Central requests a female officer to respond to a rape and robbery at 129 West Seventy-sixth. Request is acknowledged by Unit 243, Lieutenant Marty Shugrue himself, who's returning to the Twentieth with Detective Jessica Taylor. Brendan and I decide to join them.

Traffic is heavy, so we hit the siren and cut through Fourteenth Street to the West Side. Arrive about 3:55. A squad car and an unmarked car are double-parked in front. Two uniform cops are exiting the building. We double-park, jump out, identify ourselves.

"You're wasting your time," the taller cop tells us. "They refused to let us in, they'll only talk to a policewoman. She's inside now, sixth floor back, apartment D. Lieutenant Shugrue's in the hallway."

Take the elevator to six, walk down the hall, Marty's standing outside the apartment door. Smiles when he sees us.

"You guys don't miss much," he says.

"What's happening?" Brendan asks.

Shakes his head. "Seems our man got two for the price of one this time. Two young lesbians. They wouldn't let the uniform cops in, wouldn't even let me in. Jessica's been in there maybe fifteen minutes. Stepped out just a couple of minutes ago, said it's our man. He hurt one of them; she's called an ambulance."

"She show them the sketch?" I ask.

"Yeah. Positive. No question."

"Anybody call headquarters?"

"Not yet."

"We're on our way down," Brendan says. "We'll tell the chief. He's gonna love this, just before his press conference."

"Got a kit to dust the place?" I ask.

"She's got it in there."

"See you downtown."

Get down to headquarters about 4:20. Call Mat Murphy from the front security desk, find out the chief's already in the auditorium, backstage. Off we go to the auditorium. Must be a slow news day, place is jammed with warm bodies, bright lights, TV cameras, cables, Grady must've laid it on real thick. Go backstage. Chief's at a table in the corner, going over last-minute script revisions with Grady.

"Chief," I say.

"Yeah?" Looks up quickly; he's wearing a light layer of pancake makeup.

"Add two more victims."

"What?"

"Mr. Burns hit two roommates this afternoon."

"Oh, Christ. Sure it's the same guy?"

"Positive ID of the sketch. Lieutenant Shugrue's handling it with Detective Taylor. They'll be down soon."

Chief groans, crosses out a number in the script, revises it. "Jesus, that makes *twelve!* Twelve in less than a *month!* And all we got is a fuckin' little piss-ass *sketch!*"

I shrug. "Chief, we're bustin' our chops."

"Bustin' your—?! Meeting in my office five o'clock sharp! Round up everybody from the team you can find! We gotta drop this fucker fast!"

Brendan and I don't have the pleasure of viewing the press conference live, but we'll catch the best parts on TV later. Up we go to Mat Murphy's office, get on the phone, try to round up members of the special assignment team (fanned out all over the city, of course, on all three shifts) who can possibly make it to headquarters by five o'clock. Worst possible time, rush-hour traffic, but we come up with eight guys who say they'll try.

None of them make it in time, but Lieutenant Shugrue is there, introduces us to Detective Jessica Taylor. Unexpected pleasure in more ways than one. Taylor is a positive knockout, one of the classiest and most eloquent policewomen I've encountered in twenty-eight years on the force. Dark-eyed brunette, about five-seven, maybe 120, fashionably dressed, little makeup. Know her by reputation, of course: 1973 graduate of the John Jay College of Criminal Justice, she's been in the department nine years, figure her to be around thirty-one. All kinds of citations, excellent undercover lady. Divorced, but you can't win 'em all.

Five o'clock sharp we sit at the conference table, Brendan and me opposite Shugrue and Taylor. Chief's sweating like a pig now, pancake makeup makes a highly visible ring around the collar. Turns on his tape recorder, sits back, asks Miss Taylor to read her notes.

Taylor's voice is calm and cool, she looks around at us as she speaks, consults her notes only occasionally. "We arrived at the apartment at three forty-four P.M. Central had requested a policewoman and we were in the area. We met two uniformed officers in the hallway who had responded to the initial call. They said the complainants, both female, would only talk with a policewoman. I identified myself to the women, they allowed me to enter; Lieutenant Shugrue waited outside the door. Complainants were one Gale Jennings, white/twenty-two, a law student at Columbia, and Laura Warren, white/twenty-three, a journalism student at Columbia. Both had been assaulted. At one-fifteen P.M., Miss Jennings was alone in the apartment when she received a phone call from a Mr. James Burns of Manhattan Mutual Insurance; he asked for Miss Warren. MO virtually identical to the others—I've read Lieutenant Shugrue's files. Jennings fell for the ploy. The building has no doorman. Burns rang from the lobby, identified himself, Jennings buzzed him in. After the two-signature routine at the door, she allowed him to enter. At gunpoint, he forced her to undress. He also undressed. Jennings was being subjected to forced fellatio in the bedroom when her roommate, Miss Warren, entered the apartment and called her name. Jennings was forced to call Warren into the bedroom. When Warren entered, Burns pointed the gun at her and ordered her to strip. At this point, the victims explained that they were in fact lesbians. They told Burns to take whatever he wanted, but to leave them alone. Apparently Burns was very intrigued by their sexual preferences. After forcing Warren to strip, he ordered her to lie on the floor on her back. He then ordered Jennings and Warren to engage in simultaneous cunnilingus. While this was in progress, Burns sodomized Jennings. When Jennings began to scream with the pain, he cocked the gun, placed it against her head, and said, quote: Nothing would give me greater pleasure than to blow your brains out, unquote. After he ejaculated, he made them lie face-down on the floor, cut the telephone cord, tied them back-to-back, gagged them with their pants and bras. He emptied their handbags, got about a hundred and fifty in cash, didn't bother with their jewelry. Before leaving, he wiped everything clean with a towel; I didn't bother to dust for prints. Miss Jennings suffered a lacerated sphincter muscle and was bleeding rather badly. I called an ambulance. Both victims gave me a positive ID on the sketch. They promised to cooperate, but will deal only with me."

"Excellent," Chief says softly. "Excellent, Taylor. For the first time, we have corroboration that'll stand up in court." Leans forward. "Understand you interviewed Miss Ballanger, too."

"Yes, sir. I talked with her alone for almost an hour."

"Just the bottom line. How bad was it?"

Taylor tosses her notebook on the table. "Miss Ballanger had a very bad ordeal. Beaten first, tied, gagged, blindfolded. Repeatedly raped, sodomized, subjected to a variety of sadomasochistic routines. She's under the care of a psychiatrist."

Chief looks at us. "Makes you wonder what the hell kind of animal we're dealing with here."

"A sick animal," Taylor says quietly. "One who needs to be caged quickly. Before he kills somebody."

Pleasant autumn evening, nice chill in the air, we stop in a bar just a block away from headquarters, Brendan and me, Marty and Jessica, have a taste, watch the Channel 2 local news. About 6:20, before a commercial break, they announce: "Coming up, Chris Borgen reports on the city-wide manhunt for a mass-rapist." We know Borgen, we've worked with him on several occasions, good people, retired NYPD detective who made the big time; couldn't happen to a nicer guy.

Now he comes on, medium shot, familiar dark hair and eyes, press conference behind him: "Over the past four weeks, a total of twelve rapes in Manhattan and the Bronx are believed to be the work of a single individual, according to Chief of Detectives Walter Vadney." Closeup of Vadney, sweating: "The subject is a white male, mid-thirties, approximately six feet tall, one hundred eighty-five pounds, brown hair, blue eyes." Composite sketch flashes on. Now Vadney's voice-over surprises me: "A reward of ten thousand dollars has been offered by a concerned citizen for information leading to the arrest and conviction of this man." Superimposed at the bottom of the sketch: $10,000 REWARD. "We've set up a special telephone number that will be manned twenty-four hours a day; all information will be held in strict confidence." Now they super the telephone number. Chief goes on to give the basic MO, they show the sketch again, super the reward and phone number, then it's question-and-answer time.

Borgen: "Chief, do you have any solid leads at this time?"

Vadney: "Like I said, Chris, we have our most experienced men assigned to the investigation. Lieutenant Shugrue, supervising the special-assignment team, informs me that his men are now pursuing a couple of promising leads."

Marty chokes on his drink, has a brief coughing spasm. Heads turn (joint is filled with detectives, as usual). He waits for Borgen's report to end, glances around, speaks to me quietly: "Leads, huh?"

"Promising leads," I remind him.

"Full-grown fuckin' asshole. Why's he *do* that to me!"

"Man has total confidence in you."

"Man's a total moron."

"What's the reward all about?"

Marty smiles, takes a sip. "New development, John. Seems one of the Bronx seven—one who initially refused to cooperate—seems her attorney talked to Vadney this afternoon. Offers a reward of ten thousand dollars. The money's in escrow right now."

"What gives?"

"Her name's Angela Petrocelli. Word on the street in the Bronx, she's a relative of Tito Petrocelli, a lieutenant in the Gambino family."

I give a low whistle.

He nods. "Nice gentleman, Tito. I ran into him a couple of years ago on a heavy loansharking case that involved plenty of busted kneecaps. Mr. Burns has bigger problems than he realizes. When we drop him and put him in the can, it'll be like delivering him to the slaughterhouse."

Before we split and go home, Jessica tells us something she didn't include in her brief verbal report to the chief. During her interview with Gale Jennings and Laura Warren, they both mentioned that he called them "Lessies." That happens to be a term used so widely within the department that it's become almost generic.

At home that night, after watching the ball game (Orioles won 4-1 to even the World Series at one game each), Catherine and

I are in bed catching up on our reading, magazines mostly, when I glance at the cover of *Time,* issue of September 5, 1983. Cover story is titled "Private Violence," and breaks down into three categories: Child Abuse, Wife Beating, and Rape. I flip to the story on rape, find it intriguing, informative, and about as up-to-date as you can get. When I finish it, I go back and reread certain sections. I'm primarily a robbery detective, I don't get into many rape cases, they're usually handled by our specialized sex crime units, so the up-to-date research here is interesting. Frankly, some of it surprises me. For example, I didn't realize that rape is now considered a crime of violence, not passion. I didn't know that most rapists are not sexually deprived. I had no idea of the length of time required for rape victims to return to normal, if they ever do, or the wide range of serious aftershocks.

Before going to sleep, I can't help but think about our subject, Mr. Burns, and the composite sketch. From all accounts, he's relatively young, unusually good-looking, and eloquent enough to be quite persuasive. Certain questions stand out in my mind: Why would he be a sadistic animal with Belinda Ballanger but decide not to touch Dawn Harkness? Why does he rob his victims in Manhattan but not in the Bronx? Why does he limit his activities to early afternoons and weekdays only? If he's in enforcement, as the holsters seem to indicate, or ever was in enforcement, why haven't any of the witnesses been able to select even one ID photograph from the many thousands they've seen? And, finally, now that his description, basic MO, and composite sketch have appeared on TV and will be featured in tomorrow's papers, will he have enough control of himself to stop? My guess is no.

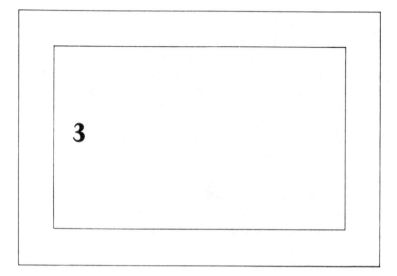

3

THURSDAY MORNING, October 13, we get an object lesson in the awesome power of the press (as if we needed one) when we find out from headquarters that the special telephone number has been ringing off the hook all night long. This is long before the early editions of the newspapers hit the streets with stories of the manhunt and the composite sketch. From 6:30 P.M. Wednesday to 6:45 A.M. today, a total of 139 calls have been answered; all conversations were taped. People out there are genuinely concerned and want to help, but cuckoos are in the majority and with the $10,000 reward we know they'll be singing from clocks all over town. Example: One nice young lady says the sketch looks exactly like her brother, a Catholic priest who left the order after eight years and might be trying to make up for lost time. Every lead has to be checked out, of course, so starting today virtually every detective on the special-assignment team (forty now, counting Jessica) is on the street. Within the next eight hours, Brendan and I interview seven concerned citizens of this great city of ours. All but two of them are loosely wrapped. We also check out five young men who bear at least passing resemblance to the sketch. Negative.

That night, one suspect is actually busted by cops in the 107th Precinct in Queens. Clean-cut as they come, married, bunch of kids, Vietnam vet, works as an accountant in a Wall Street brokerage firm. He's partying with friends, hits a couple of after-hours joints on the East Side, teams up with some gal, takes her to the Travelers' Motel on Queens Boulevard. All goes well until he tries to hit her in the seat. She screams, he punches her, she bites his hand, hangs on like a mad dog, management calls the police. Cops arrive, man gives them a hard time, has to be subdued, gets a fat lip to go with his half-eaten fingers. Turns out to be a ringer for the sketch. He's booked for sodomy and simple assault, but now a hasty lineup is arranged, he's represented by a real ball-breaker attorney. Make a long story short, the only victim who makes a positive ID is wearing Coke-bottle eyeglasses, a candidate for Braille School, and she wasn't wearing them during the rape. Man's now suing the city for millions. As Louie Armstrong used to say, "If you have to ask what jazz is, you'll never know."

Get our first real break Monday, October 17. At Lieutenant Shugrue's request, Chief calls a small meeting in his office, 10:30 A.M., just Marty and Jessica, Brendan and me. Marty explains that one of the officers assigned to answer the special telephone number has identified three calls from the same individual: Saturday night, Sunday morning, and Sunday night. Now Marty places his own tape recorder on the conference table, asks us to listen to the first message. It's a young lady's voice. Soft and sincere.

I think I know who your rapist is. I don't want your reward and I don't want to get involved. He was once a nice person, but now he's sick. He's your brother.

Marty clicks off the machine. "The officer who answered this first call didn't pay much attention to it. He figured it was just another whacko, and he's heard plenty. Luckily, the same detective took the third call Sunday night. Then, strictly on his own time, he went back and played all the calls taped by the other shifts, Sunday morning and afternoon. Found the second call that way. The caller's message is essentially the same on all three, and she hung up on all three before she could be engaged in conversation. The more I've listened to her, the more sincere she sounds. This girl is trying to tell us something important: 'He's your brother.' "

Chief narrows his eyes. "She sayin' he's on the job?"

"Matter of fact, Chief, we've tossed it around, the four of us here. We seem to come back to that possibility all the time. Still, every witness who's cooperated has now gone through every uniform and detective ID section in the city and come up empty. Could it be a cop in Jersey, Connecticut, Nassau, Suffolk?"

"Good question." Chief makes a note of it. "I'll contact Nassau and Suffolk first, see what they can do for us."

"Chief," I say, "we feel Dawn Harkness is still our best witness. We've had her at BCI with negative results, but she's never seen ID photos of anybody in the department. Let me make a suggestion: Before we go off on a tangent to Nassau, Suffolk, whatever, let's give it our best shot with the kid. Brendan and I have already discussed this. Why not do it through the Internal Affairs Division of each agency? We know their files are up to date, we know every photo of everybody on the job is there. Say the guy is a cop. It wouldn't be too difficult for him to lift his photo from our ID section—or have somebody else lift it. On the other hand, doing that at Internal Affairs is like trying your luck at Fort Knox. Brendan and I could contact Correction, Housing, Transit, and our own job, explain the situation, and request that our witness be allowed to view the photos."

Chief shakes his head. "Not a chance, John. These people would piss on your request. I'll make the necessary arrangements personally through this office. Give me a time."

"Tomorrow morning," Brendan says. "We'll call Mrs. Harkness, ask her to keep Dawn home from school."

"Set it up," Chief says. "Now, Marty, on the telephone lead. If this lady calls again, we've got to try and convince her to give us more details. Personally, I share your gut feeling about her. I think she knows exactly who he is and where he is. Pass the word around the telephone shifts, familiarize the men with her voice. We need a break in a hurry. Spoke with Commissioner Reilly early this morning, he's on a real bummer. Henry Ballanger's daughter is now in a private psychiatric institution in Westchester County. She refuses to see or speak to anybody —parents, relatives, friends, not even her fiancé. Kid's in pretty bad shape."

Soon as the meeting breaks up, Brendan calls Mrs. Harkness, tells her we're on to something good, asks her to please keep Dawn home from school tomorrow, at least for the morning session. Says we'll pick her up at 8:00 A.M. and take her to Brooklyn to view some photos.

Next, we grab a few of the calls from Manhattan and hit the street. First stop is 410 East Sixty-second Street where the doorman, Emilio Cruz, swears the rapist lives in apartment 12-A with his wife, a real nice lady. Up we go, identify ourselves, explain that we received an anonymous phone call, da-da, could we speak with her husband. She laughs. Her husband's a ship's engineer, he's been abroad for more than a month now, last she heard from him was Friday, he called from Hong Kong. Now she gets out a photo album, shows us some recent shots. This guy resembles the sketch, but he's got a series of tatoos on both arms. We apologize for the intrusion. She understands.

As we get off the elevator in the lobby, Emilio Cruz rushes up to us: "Wha' happen? He get away?"

"You ever hear of Cervantes?" Brendan asks him.

"Cervantes? Sure."

"Just remember what he said: '*Muchos pocos hacen un mucho.*'"

Cruz frowns up at him, dark eyes looking like E.T.

"Keep that in mind," Brendan says.

Cruz nods, hesitates. "'*Muchos pocos—*'"

"That's right. And don't you forget it. *Adiós.*"

We walk up the street, I glance back, Cruz is standing by the door with a puzzled expression. Seems to be mouthing the words.

"So what's it mean?" I ask.

"Exact translation: 'Many a pickle makes a mickle.'"

I can't help laughing. "Cervantes said that, huh?"

"Yeah. Cervantes Rodriguez. Played third base for Albany."

"Remember him well. Led the league in stolen sweatshirts."

"Now you got him."

Where to next? Brendan checks the list. Here's one from a waitress on the East Side, wouldn't give her name, says a guy fitting the description hangs in the singles bars on First Avenue, she mentions Maxwell's Plum, Tittle Tattle, and Friday's. Thinks his name is Ray or Ron. Maxwell's Plum is only a few blocks away, Sixty-fourth and First. It's a beautiful afternoon, so we walk over there.

Naturally, these places are pretty dead this time of day, we'll probably have to come back, but we show the sketch to the staff at Maxwell's anyway. Negative. Brendan suggests Friday's next, a cousin of his is a night bartender there, Jerry Robinson, sharp guy, good friend of our job. We used to stop in occasionally; pace got too much for us in our old age. We introduce ourselves to the manager, have the sketch passed around to the help. Zero. Brendan asks if Jerry's working tonight. Manager says yes, he should be in soon to prep the bar for the happy hour. A waitress says she just saw him going into the OTB office up the block. We walk up there, meet him on his way out.

Jerry's a big affable guy, about six-four, maybe 210, mid-forties, mop of blonde hair, neck like a bull. Started as a bouncer, worked his way up. After the usual friendly insults, we invite him back to Friday's for a fast one. He escorts us to a nice little booth in the corner, where else? We show him the sketch, explain about the telephone call.

"She says he frequents the strip," Brendan tells him. "She thinks his name is Ray or Ron."

Jerry studies the sketch, sips his drink. "There was a Ron, looks something like him, used to be a regular. Usually came in with another guy, very Italian looking, mustache, beard, never did get his name. If Ron's the same guy, he was quite the ladies' man. I can't imagine this guy stealin' pussy with a pistol."

"Hang with any particular girl?" I ask.

He thinks about it. "Yeah. Yeah, there was one gal he went with for a while there. What the hell was her name? I think —I think her name was Toni. Toni something. That's right, Toni, she was a stew with United. Reason I remember, Billy Craig, the other night man here, he was dating her roommate. Maybe Billy can help. I have to call him about something else anyway, I'll find out for you."

Jerry goes to make the call, returns shortly, hands us a slip of paper: "Toni Walthrup & Susan Lewisohn, 501 E. 78, apt. 17-G. Tel. 585-1723."

We thank him, go to the car, drive to York and Seventy-eighth. Identify ourselves to the doorman, tell him we want to speak with Miss Toni Walthrup. He rings the apartment, speaks to Miss Lewisohn, we're asked to come up. An attractive young brunette opens the door a crack, leaves the chain on, asks to see our identification. We show our gold, introduce ourselves. She unlocks the chain, asks us inside.

"Can't be too careful these days," she says. "I'm Susan

Lewisohn, Toni's in the shower, she'll be out in a minute. She just got in from L.A. about an hour ago."

She shows us into the living room. Relatively small but bright, white walls holding aluminum-framed prints and posters. Windows face west, so the afternoon sunlight slants in to show the colorful flower patterns in a long L-shaped couch flanked by two matching armchairs. In the center are two small glass-and-chrome coffee tables.

Couple of minutes later, Toni comes into the room in a pink terrycloth robe, dark hair tied in a towel, face tanned. She's about five-seven and well proportioned. We go through the introductions, assure her she's not in any trouble, we just want to ask a few routine questions. At this point, Susan Lewisohn leaves the room.

We sit down, Brendan shows her the sketch, asks her if it resembles anyone she knows.

"No, I really can't say that it does."

"What about a guy named Ron?" Brendan asks. "We understand you dated him a few times—in Friday's?"

"Oh, Ron." She frowns at the sketch. "Yes, I suppose it does look a little like him."

"Can you tell us anything about him?" I ask.

She leans forward, takes a cigarette from a glass box on the coffee table and picks up a lighter. "You're from Internal Affairs, aren't you?"

Brendan and I exchange glances.

"No, we're not," I tell her quietly. "We're from the Nineteenth Squad, like I said. We're investigating a series of rapes in Manhattan and the Bronx. The man in the sketch resembles the rapist. That's why we're here."

"A rapist?" She laughs softly, shakes her head. "Oh, God, no. Never. The man I dated is a cop, a great guy, family life a little screwed up, but a rapist? Never."

"Miss Walthrup," Brendan says, just above a whisper. "We don't care whether he's a cop or a priest. The guy we're looking for is bad, real bad."

She nods, shrugs, lights the cigarette.

"Do you know his last name?" I ask.

"He told me Matthews, but I never really believed it. Married guys are like that. I'm sure his first name was Ron because the guys he worked with called him that."

"Can you remember their names?" Brendan asks.

"Just first names: Larry, I think Larry was his partner, and Kevin was another guy I met once or twice."

"Did they discuss where they worked?" I ask.

"No, he said he never brought the job home with him."

"Was he a New York City cop?" Brendan asks.

"Yes, I'm pretty sure about that. He talked about the Housing and Transit police possibly merging with them and he didn't like the idea at all."

"Ever talk about his family?" I ask. "Or where he lived?"

"He lived upstate somewhere. The town, I don't know. I don't think he ever mentioned it. His family, yes, he talked about them. He was getting divorced and he was getting very uptight about it. His wife had him followed, even had him photographed with other girls. He was—" She hesitates, takes a long drag on the cigarette, exhales slowly. "He was terribly mixed up, y'know? He loved his children and wanted the marriage to last for their sakes. My honest opinion is that the guy just wasn't meant for marriage. Even when we were on a date, he was always looking, he had an almost insatiable appetite for girls."

"When did you see him last?" Brendan asks.

"Maybe six, seven weeks ago. I suppose I went out with him about four or five times. I really think you guys are wasting your time on him. Believe me, he's just not the type to go around raping people. Why should he? He could walk in any bar and have almost any girl he wanted. He's that good-looking. That's a fact."

Toni's not willing to look at photos, she has only good memories of him. If he's the rapist, she doesn't want to know and she certainly doesn't want to get involved in nailing him.

Driving back to the precinct, we both have a gut feeling that we might finally be on to something significant. We know exactly what to do next, we're going to follow through all the way. But how do you figure this guy? Here he is, tagging the best-looking stuff on the East Side, the crème de la crème, and then knocking on doors and taking whatever happens to be inside, at gunpoint.

Back to the precinct, 4:10 P.M., Lieutenant Barnett relays a message from Chief Vadney's office: Girl raped and murdered in Yonkers. Chief's up there now with Marty. Yonkers PD has a female witness and reason to believe it's our man again. Sit tight for orders. While we're waiting, I get on the phone, run the name Ron Matthews through the Chief Clerk's office. There was a Ronald Matthews on the job from 1923 to 1946; hardly our guy. Brendan calls Internal Affairs, confirms that Vadney set up a photo-viewing session for us tomorrow morning at 8:30 with Dawn Harkness; now he tells them to narrow the field considerably, pull only the ID photos of white males with the first name Ron or Ronald. Will do.

Marty Shugrue calls me from Yonkers about 4:30. They've questioned the witness and shown her the sketch. Positive ID. Her name is Cathy Giroux. Brief rundown: Late last night Giroux and girl friend Donna Uris were drinking in a place called Jimmy's on McLean Avenue. They're both eighteen and live in the adjoining Woodlawn section of the Bronx. About 2:30 A.M., they call a cab and go outside to wait. Few minutes later, a man in a black Mazda pulls up and asks where they're headed. They tell him 234th Street and Katonah Avenue. He says he's going that way, opens a door. Man's got a couple of suitcases on the back seat, so Cathy gets in front, Donna in back. Takes about five minutes to get to 234th Street. When he stops, Cathy gets out; he asks Donna to hand him something from the back seat. Suddenly, he floors the accelerator, squeals off toward 235th, hangs a sharp right. Cathy screams for help and a couple of guys come running out of the

Eagle's Nest, a pub on the corner, but the black Mazda's long gone. They call the cops, describe the car and its occupants; New York plates, but Cathy couldn't get the number. Around 6:15 this morning, a guy walking his dog in Tibbet's Brook Park discovers the body, naked and bruised. Yonkers PD and ME respond. She was raped, beaten and strangled. Cathy Giroux is contacted and makes the identification. Cop from the Forty-seventh Precinct, name of Kalski, who drives her to and from the scene, gets a good description of the guy, bells start ringing. He calls it in to Chief Vadney's office immediately. Good sharp kid.

I give Shugrue a brief rundown on the "Ron" lead, tell him we think we're on to something, explain what's on tap tomorrow morning at IAD. He says it sounds good, he'll brief the chief. Tells us to go home, we'll have a long day tomorrow.

On the train home to Bellmore that evening, I'm smoking a cigar, reading about the murder in the *Post,* finally looking out at the little towns of Nassau County, and I'm thinking: Rape and robbery are one thing, now we're dealing with a murderer. A murderer who may very well be a cop, experienced in covering his tracks. A sick man who's getting worse by the day. And I know from experience that, just like his first rape, this guy's not about to stop.

Now I go back to reading the paper and I get into an article that really blows my mind. This story is difficult to believe, even when you've been a cop as long as me, but it's true.

Killer's confessions
lead investigators
on trail of murder

By Fred Grimm

Monroe, La.—The horrors crafted by Henry Lee Lucas and Ottis Elwood Toole remain incalculable.

No one knows how many women were abducted, raped, murdered and mutilated by the short, unkempt, one-eyed drifter and his blond, pyromaniac lover. Not even Lucas.

"Henry Lee has given us details of about 150 murders," said Texas Ranger Phil Ryan. "Some of the details overlap. He's hazy on others. He says he may have killed as many as 300. He didn't keep records. He doesn't remember all of them."

Since his arrest for a firearms violation last fall, Lucas has pleaded guilty to the murder of one Texas woman and has been charged with killing nine others. He is charged with a murder in Monroe, La., and five in Jacksonville, Fla.

Police say they have enough evidence to charge the itinerant handyman with two more slayings in Monroe and five more in Jacksonville. They claim he and Toole, 38, have been connected to 97 random, unplanned slayings committed in eight states during the last six years.

"I told my wife that if we could find out what happened to Kate Rich, we might solve some of the roadside murders we've had in West Texas," said Montague County, Tex., Sheriff W.F. Conway. "Never thought, though, that we'd find something bad as this guy."

Conway had suspected Lucas might have had something to do with the abrupt disappearance of 80-year-old Kate Rich last September from the tiny village of Stoneburg (population 51) when he arrested Lucas for possessing a .22-caliber pistol. Conway had learned that Lucas was a convicted felon, with a record of auto theft, burglary and the 1960 murder of his 74-year-old mother.

Lucas was taken to the Montague County Jail Oct. 17, 1982. That evening he looked up at his jailer and uttered, "Joe Don, I've done some bad things."

That understatement began a string of confessions so tantalizing to lawmen that last week 90 officers from 19 states and the FBI convened in Monroe to sort out the murders. "Welcome Homicide Task Force," read the marquee on the Holiday Inn that hosted the macabre three-day convention.

The cops came with their files of unsolved murders, mostly Jane Doe bodies found alongside country roads. They watched videotapes of conversations with Lucas, 47, with untrimmed sideburns, dark oily hair pushed back into a sloppy ducktail and with the right side of his face scrunched up around an ill-fitting glass eye.

They watched as Lucas—a man with average, maybe below average intelligence—described stabbing the 15-year-old girl he identified as his commonlaw wife, a Jacksonville girl named Freida Powell, in August 1982. "After that I cut her up in little teeny pieces and stuffed her in three pillow cases. All except her legs."

One dreadful, detailed confession followed another. The cops played mix and match, trying to trace the meandering, murderous journeys of Lucas, who was loosely based in Jacksonville until he and Powell wandered into tiny Stoneburg in 1981.

The confessions went beyond telling of shooting, stabbing and strangling. Lucas stoically told of mutilating the victims, then having sexual relations with the bodies. Tough, veteran homicide detectives found themselves suppressing shudders.

"I've been a policeman for 26 years and I've never seen anything like this guy. He's atrocious," said Lt. Vince Richardson of Mobile, Ala.

"He's a demon," said Detective Pat Haley of Livingston Parish in South Louisiana as he emerged from one videotape session.

"If there was ever an argument for the death penalty, it's Lucas," said Ryan, the Texas Ranger.

"I've spent more hours talking to Lucas and Toole than I have with my own family this last year," said Detective Buddy Terry of the Jacksonville Metro Police. He said Lucas talked of killings "all over Florida," including two, maybe four in Miami.

"You sit down with Lucas and he describes these things without remorse. Just like you and I talking," Terry said. "After a while, it gets to you. You think, 'Why me? Why do I have to deal with him?' "

The credibility in the Lucas case comes from the details, complete with mutilations and descriptions of his funereal lust. He has led investigators to four bodies. He described other murders that match up with old reports, such as the 1981 dumping of a hitchhiker's body in Hale County, Tex., and her head in Scottsdale, Ariz.

Lucas' necrophilia rituals, unspeakable acts, apparently established a certain unique pattern in the murders. But investigators were reluctant to share evidence.

What physical evidence that links him to the murders—ballistics, fingerprints, documentation of his whereabouts, recovery of property of the victims—is not known publicly.

Texas cops are laboring under a court gag order. Terry said he wouldn't talk much until after he takes his five cases to a Jacksonville grand jury next week. And in Monroe, a small city in northeast Louisiana, lead investigator Joe Cummings said, "The families of these girls have gone through enough without this other stuff getting in the newspapers."

Terry did share one constant detail in the Lucas murders. "I asked him if he has any morals at all. He said he never steals from the victims. He never takes their money or their jewelry." . . .

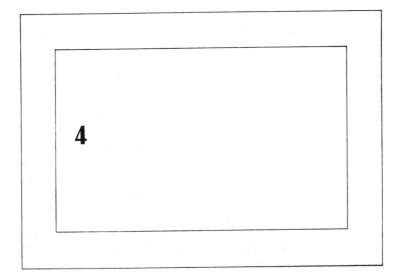

4

TUESDAY, OCTOBER 18, 8:05 A.M., Brendan and I pick up Dawn Harkness and head for the Eighty-fourth Precinct on Poplar Street in Brooklyn, headquarters of IAD. On the way, we ask her to reflect back on her bad experience: his face, eyes, nose, chin, mouth, anything that would set him apart. Arrive about 8:35. We're escorted by a young lieutenant to their Identification Section. He introduces us to a Detective Benchley who will "take care of our needs." Can't help thinking these young fucks draw the same paycheck we do every month. This kid looks to be about twenty-one, peach fuzz on his face, gold detective shield pinned on his chest—enough to make you want to throw up. Cops out there with commendations up the ass, putting their lives on the line every day of the week, and most of them don't have a hope in hell of ever getting a gold shield. How does it happen? Very easy.

Starts when a new class enters the Police Academy. During the first couple of weeks, every new recruit is individually interviewed by an investigator from Internal Affairs. The topic: "Corruption and how to combat it." He gives them a brief rundown on the statistics: Cops fired, jailed, and those who commit suicide under severe pressure. He explains that the possibility of becoming a detective is extremely slight. However, a young recruit willing to become a covert Field Representative for IAD after graduation would have an excellent chance for early promotion. He gives each recruit a telephone number to call if the kid is interested. The guys who call are further interviewed by a lieutenant at a designated rendezvous and told exactly what would be expected when they're assigned to their first command. In effect, the rookie would become the eyes and ears of IAD at his precinct, calling in anything he observed to be a violation of the rules and procedures of the department. This includes everything from cops accepting gratuities such as a cup of coffee, a sandwich, a drink, a bottle of booze at Christmas, all the way up to cops soliciting and accepting cash bribes; from cops who "coop" (catnap) on the midnight tours, to those who have a few cold ones in the car. Even if it's your partner, you're expected to report the smallest violation. Following that interview, when the lieutenant is convinced he has a good candidate for the job, he sets up an interview with the Commanding Officer of IAD. At this point the new recruit is given a code name known only to the C.O. Every time the kid drops a dime on a brother officer, the information is credited to his code name. When the C.O. reviews his rat file and sees who is producing in the field, he rewards the best rat with a transfer to IAD and a detective's gold shield. Only then do the officers in his precinct find out who the rat was. Now he graduates to the heavier stuff, police corruption in gambling, narcotics, whatever. We all realize IAD is a necessity, particularly in a department this large, someone has to weed out the bad apples, but the average cop on the street finds IAD's methods hard to digest.

Back to Tuesday morning. Another young detective arrives, opens a large iron gate, directs us to a table holding a narrow steel drawer full of ID photos. Informs us there are pictures. of 104 white male officers with the first name of Ron or Ronald. We sit down, he asks if we'd like coffee and donuts. We accept, he leaves to get them. Brendan whispers, "Take back all you were thinkin' about these humps, maybe they *are* human!"

We instruct Dawn to take her time on every photo; if she sees anything that's even close, pull it and put it on the side. She looks bright-eyed and lovely in the early morning, dark hair freshly washed and lustrous, wears a gray crew-neck sweater over a blue shirt, tight-fitting designer jeans, blue Adidas. She studies each photo carefully, takes frequent breaks for sips of coffee. Twenty-five minutes later, she's about halfway through when she hesitates, lifts a photo from the file, hands it to me.

I speak softly. "This guy's got a beard, Dawn."

"It's him. I'm positive. It's his face."

Brendan takes a look. "Okay, let's put it to one side and go ahead with the others."

"No," she says decisively. "That's him. That's the man."

I turn the photo over, read the back:

> LASLO, RONALD DRAKE
> W/M; D.O.B. 5/25/47
> 5'-11"; 187 lbs.; Brn. hair; Bl. eyes
> Date of Appointment: 8/5/69

Turn the card over, study his face. Guy has a full beard and long hair. Doesn't really bear a strong resemblance to the sketch, except for the eyes and nose.

"Hate to ask you again, Dawn, but we have to be sure."

"That's the man. I'm positive."

Brendan goes to the iron gate, calls the young detective over, asks for the complete file on Ronald Drake Laslo. Kid says he'll have to check with the lieutenant. Comes back, tells us he's been instructed to make a Xerox copy for us. We drink our coffee and wait.

"Ever been down here before?" Brendan asks me.

"Yeah. Couple of times. Complete bullshit. You?"

"Yeah, once. Didn't amount to anything."

Can't help smiling. "Guess if you never made the trip down here, you never did anything worth shit in this job."

We're given a folder with a copy of Laslo's complete file and a copy of the photo. We head back uptown to Dawn's apartment. Brendan drives, I read the file. A few highlights: Ronald Drake Laslo, born Los Angeles, California, May 25, 1947. Son of Robert A. and Joanne M. Laslo. Father's occupation, musician; mother's a former actress. Education: Venice High School, Venice, California; two years at Hunter College, New York City. U.S. Army, 1964–1966, Vietnam. Married Angela Margaret Gallo, June 22, 1967. Children: Leslie Ann (July 19, 1970), James Drake (September 2, 1972). Entered Police Academy, February 1969, graduated August 1969. Assigned to Forty-second Precinct, Bronx. Transferred to Public Morals Division, Manhattan South, September 1973. Transferred to Fourth Division Narcotics (undercover assignment), January 1979. Transferred to Bronx Robbery Squad, August 1981. Marital status: Divorced. Commendations, fourteen. Member, Honor Legion. No complaints on his record, nothing. Squeaky clean.

Comprehensive file, only one item missing, but it happens to be critical: IAD knows he's divorced, but they have no present address on him.

Drop Dawn off at her apartment, 1:55, thank her, tell her we'd like to take her out to dinner some evening, promise it won't be McDonald's. Stop off at the precinct, call Chief Vadney, fill him in. He calls a meeting in his office for 11:30 sharp, just the two of us: "I want your report typed up clean, Rawlings. Exhibit A, the full IAD file on Laslo. Presentation folders, the works, y'read me?"

Loud and clear. Brendan and me are sitting at his conference table 11:30 sharp, I hand him his copy in the NYPD-blue
Duo-Tang presentation folder. He ignores my report, flips
immediately to Exhibit A in back. When he sees the photo of
Laslo, he blinks, frowns, makes a low sound in his throat.

"Rawlings, is this—? What's this, some kinda *joke?*"

"No, sir."

"This guy looks like a fuckin' *chimpanzee!*"

"Chief, that's him," Brendan says. "That's our man. The
kid's positive. And she's our best witness."

He shakes his head, studies the photo. "Well, that explains
it. Now we know why the other witnesses passed him by.
Rawlings, you got the complete case file with you?"

"Yes, sir."

He grabs the telephone. "Give me the date and time of each
occurrence." He calls Lieutenant Prashker, commander of the
Bronx Robbery Squad. From the conversation, we can tell
Prashker doesn't want to believe it, says the man's a super cop,
was scheduled to get the gold shield in November. Call lasts
maybe twenty minutes, the chief takes very careful notes.

Now he hangs up, turns to us. "Here's what we got. On each
occurrence in the Bronx, Laslo was working; on each occurrence in Manhattan, he had DA assignments at Leonard
Street on an old narcotics case. He took a couple of weeks'
vacation starting last Friday. Prashker says the guy got divorced recently and has a lot of loose ends to clean up. Apparently he's now shacked up with some bimbo in Manhattan.
Now, here's what I want you guys to do. Write this down.
First, go down to Leonard Street, check with the Narcotics
Division of the DA's office, establish exactly what hours Laslo
was actually working there. Second, check the book in the
sign-out room; see if the hours he signed in and out match up
with the hours he was actually working. Third, get up to
Yonkers, speak to his ex-wife, she may be able to help with
an address where he's shacked up now, huh? Hell has no fury

like a broad scorned, y'read me? And listen, buddy-boy, don't walk in with your hands in your pockets. Y'never know, he could be visiting."

Off we go to 155 Leonard Street, speak with the Assistant DA who worked with Laslo. He looks up the times, tells us that on the three occasions he met with the guy for trial preparation, all their business was conducted in the morning hours. Now we go down, check the book in the so-called sign-out room. On each of the three assignments, Laslo signed in at approximately 9:00 A.M. and signed out around 5:00 P.M. Bingo. That gave him all three afternoons to make his phone calls and visits.

Now, if this is our man, we understand why he raped and robbed his victims in Manhattan but wouldn't touch a dime in the Bronx. All Bronx robbery victims are brought to the Robbery Squad office, where he worked, to view mug shots of known robbers and muggers residing in the borough. Fancy him having to show mug shots to one of his victims. On the other hand, the Sex Crime Unit is in the Forty-seventh Precinct in the North Bronx, just far enough away from his office for comfort.

Phone the chief, fill him in, he's delighted. Now he decides that Marty Shugrue and Jessica Taylor should accompany us to Yonkers: "No reflection on your ability, Little John, nothing like that, it's just—well, Marty *is* supervisor of the team, after all, and Jessica could be very helpful in dealing with Mrs. Laslo, know what I mean? Now don't forget to call Yonkers PD, alert 'em, brief 'em, it's their jurisdiction. Request two of their detectives to go along. And one last thing, Little John, listen up now. If this whacko scumbag's in the house, he isn't worth getting hurt over, huh? Sign out for a couple of shotguns and some double-aught buck. Vests for everybody. If he decides to hold court in the street, take him out in a hurry."

Brief Marty and Jessica on the drive to Yonkers. About 3:15 we rendezvous with two Yonkers detectives at the Second

Precinct. Explain that we don't expect our man to be in the house, but we can't afford to fumble at this point.

Strategy is pretty standard stuff: Marty directs, Jessica and I do the advance work on the Laslo house, 210 Crane Street, drive past a couple of times, call Marty, describe the house, yard, possible escape routes. Now Marty, Brendan, and the two detectives move out, surround the place. I telephone Mrs. Laslo, identify myself, all very low-key, ask if Miss Taylor and I could come in for a short talk. No problem. At 3:45 I radio Marty: "Place is clean, we're going in."

Mrs. Angela Laslo turns out to be a little doll, blonde, blue-eyed, soft-spoken, very gracious. Her two children, Leslie, thirteen, and James, eleven, have returned from school, she's sent them upstairs with her mother, who owns the house and lives with them. We sit in the comfortably furnished living room and talk quietly.

It's absolutely inconceivable to this lady that her former husband could have committed any of the crimes we mention. She's genuinely shocked. After listening to her for a while, it's obvious that she considers him a virtual stranger today, a vastly different person from the man she married sixteen years ago. When Jessica encourages her to talk about it, she seems to loosen up a little, explains that the transition was very gradual, over a period of the last seven or eight years. Their marriage started faltering in 1979 when he was transferred to Fourth Division Narcotics; he constantly used undercover assignments to sleep with other women. She couldn't accept the life they were living and had no alternative but to sue for divorce. She had a private investigator follow him for a couple of weeks in July and the man did a decent job for her: Laslo was seeing a girl by the name of Susan Antolini, 201 East Fifty-eighth Street, Manhattan, apartment 1-B, telephone 625-8509. She has photographs of them together on the street. Apparently they planned to get married as soon as the divorce was finalized. Then, about a month ago, Miss Antolini telephoned her and actually apologized for interfering; she was also finished with him and felt they were both better off, that he was now a sick person and in need of professional help.

Mrs. Laslo doesn't know his present address. He stopped by last Friday to pick up the remainder of his belongings, but didn't say where he was going. However, she gives us the plate and make of his car, a black 1982 Mazda RX-7, New York license YXY 637. Finally, she gives us a recent photograph in which he's clean-shaven. When she shows us to the door, her eyes look frightened for the first time and her voice breaks just perceptibly.

"Will you do one favor for me?" she asks quietly.

"We'll try," Jessica says.

Mrs. Laslo pauses with her hand on the doorknob, looks down at her hand. "Now that I know what he's done, I understand what you people—what you're faced with. What you'll have to do. But could you—if it's at all possible—could you try to reason with him first?"

"That's standard," I tell her. "You know that."

She glances at me. "He's a cop. He's damaged the department. It's not an ordinary case in any sense of the word. Nobody's going to follow any standard procedures."

"Mrs. Laslo," Jessica says softly. "We'll do what we can. There are forty officers assigned to this case. We're just two of them. We can't possibly—"

"I know that. I appreciate that." She opens the door, squints in the afternoon light. "He used to be so—different. I don't know what happened. I honestly don't. After sixteen years of marriage, you think you know someone, but you don't. You find out you don't know them at all."

Back to the Second Precinct. First things first, we put out a statewide APB on the car. If it's located, Chief Vadney's office is to be notified immediately and no action taken until he arrives. Now Marty calls the chief, briefs him, requests permission for the four of us to go down and talk with Susan

Antolini on East Fifty-eighth in Manhattan. Permission granted. With enthusiasm.

At 4:55 we luck out and find a parking space near 201 East Fifty-eighth, corner of Third. Again, it's very doubtful he's here, but one never knows. Jessica doesn't have a vest, says even the light ones are too heavy for her, so Marty suggests she stay in the car this time. Brendan suggests she get one soon; it won't do anything to enhance that lovely shape, but it would at least keep her nice and warm in the winter months ahead and possibly deprive her of an inspector's funeral.

We identify ourselves to the doorman, ask about the exits from apartment 1-B. Two windows in the alleyway and one in front, all ground-level. Back to the car, Marty opens the trunk, loads up one of the shotguns, conceals it with a blanket as he hands it through the window to Jessica. "See that window on the corner next to the alley? If Laslo busts out of it, he's all yours." Now, Marty's a lieutenant, not to mention supervisor of the team, so ordinarily he'd go in with either Brendan or me, but he elects to cover the alley. Reason? Doesn't want to break up our department-famous winning combination, Mutt and Jeff. Sharp man.

We go in, ring the doorbell, hear laughter; sounds like a couple of girls. Peephole opens, a female voice asks who's there.

"Police." Brendan holds his shield in front of the peephole. "Like to have a word with Miss Antolini."

Door is opened by a tall, exquisite brunette. "I'm Susan Antolini. Please come in."

Step inside, we're introduced to her roommate, no bad-looker either, name of Polly Giardano. I ask Susan if we could speak with her alone.

"That's not necessary," she says. "Polly and I have no secrets."

We all go into the living room, sit down, they both light

cigarettes. Terrific looking Italian kids, early twenties, T-shirts and jeans. They give Brendan and me a long look as we settle down and take out our notebooks and pens.

"Miss Antolini," I start, "do you know a Ron Laslo?"

"Yes, I do. I had a—to be honest, I had a gut feeling you'd come here eventually. He's the rapist you're looking for, right?"

"He's a prime suspect, yes," I tell her. "Like to ask you a few questions if it's okay."

"Sure. I'll tell you what I know, but I won't get involved. I don't want my name mentioned. I want your guarantee on that."

"No problem," Brendan says. "What's discussed here is in strict confidence. Miss Antolini, are you the voice on the phone, telling us he's our brother?"

"Yes, that was me. The man has to be caught, he needs help."

"When did it all start?" I ask.

She sits back, takes a drag on the cigarette, exhales slowly as she thinks about it. "I met him about a year ago in Friday's, it's a singles spot at Sixty-third and First. He was the kind of guy—how can I explain it? He just stood out, even in a jam-packed bar, he was that good-looking. He worked undercover for the Fourth Division Narcotics at the time, he wore a full beard then. Shaved it off later and looked even better. He was a great talker, terribly funny, always the center of attention with the girls. I was a flight attendant for American at the time and I was going to Acapulco for a vacation. I gave him my phone number and he said he'd call me when I got back. We began dating and I'd see him as often as possible. I knew he was married, but I'd fallen for the guy. I didn't care who got hurt, I wanted him. He was—all screwed up in his marriage. He loved his kids, but bitched about his puritanical wife and her lack of understanding about his sexual appetites. About six months ago, I quit flying and took a job as a legal secretary.

At this point, he was spending more time with me than with his family. When I'd ask him about us, where we were going, he'd tell me to be patient, that everything would work out okay. Then, one afternoon about six weeks ago, I wasn't feeling well and I came home early. I opened the door and found him making love to Cynthia on the couch—she was our third roommate at the time. I threw him out and Cynthia left a couple of days later. Unfortunately, that wasn't the end of it. He called me every day to beg my forgiveness, he said *she* seduced *him!* He said he was staying with a cousin on the West Side and wanted to move in here, that we'd get married, the whole line of bullshit. I told him never, it was over, he just couldn't be trusted. Then, one evening about a month ago, I came home and he was here. I demanded the key I'd given him and he threw it on the table. I opened the door and told him to leave. He started to go, then suddenly slammed the door shut and grabbed me by the throat. He seemed to go crazy, he began crying, he dragged me into the bedroom, tore off my clothes, and raped me. I haven't seen or heard from him since."

"Can you recall the date it occurred?" I ask.

"Clearly. Tuesday, September thirteenth."

"Why didn't you contact the police?" Brendan asks.

She gives him a look. "Are you serious? The guy's practically living with me for a year, right? Now I call the police, I report that he rapes me?"

"His cousin on the West Side," Brendan says. "Know his name?"

"It's not a guy, it's a girl. I saw her once, tall blonde, also recently divorced, does a little modeling. Can't remember her name, but I have her phone number." She gets up, goes to the telephone table. "He gave it to me after the Cynthia thing. Doubt if he's still there." She opens a small book, gives us the number: 865-3961.

We thank her, leave a card with our number, go back to the

car. Driving back to the precinct, we brief Marty and Jessica. When we mention the date of the rape, September 13, Jessica starts leafing through the case file, pauses, studies a page.

"Strange," she says.

"What?" Marty asks.

"Apparently, his girl friend was the first. The next afternoon, he started his rampage in the Bronx."

Jessica calls New York Telephone Security, speaks to Roberto Sanchez, who calls her back promptly on the precinct number, standard procedure. She requests a name and address for the number 865-3961. Sanchez punches it up on the computer. It's listed to Mrs. Alice T. Kenny, 218 West Ninety-fourth Street, apartment 6-B. Marty calls the chief, relays the information. Chief's about to leave for a late meeting with Commissioner Reilly, tells us to make a few passes through the area, familiarize ourselves with the apartment house, also take a look through the garages in the vicinity, see if we can spot the car. If we come up with anything, we're to call him at the commissioner's office or, if it's late, at home.

We take four cars, head for the West Side. Turns out that 218 West Ninety-fourth is only a few doors from the building where Brendan stayed with his brother after arriving in the States from Ireland on November 12, 1957, almost twenty-six years ago. By 8:30 we've canvassed the area. Car nowhere in sight. Call the commissioner's office. Chief's gone; message for us: (1) tonight, pick up an arrest warrant for Laslo and a search warrant for the apartment; (2) tomorrow, 6:30 A.M., report to the Twentieth Precinct, Lieutenant Shugrue's office; (3) Chief Vadney will be there to supervise the raid.

And he is, along with Jerry Grady of Press Relations and his Nikon, of course. Off we go in the predawn chill, Marty and Jessica, Brendan and me, Vadney and Grady, plus two detectives from the precinct. Four cars, shotguns and vests, coffee and donuts. Appointment with destiny.

Ninety-fourth Street is dark and deserted at 6:45. Number 218 is in a row of six-story brownstones, fire escapes in back. House is quietly surrounded, roof, front, rear, fire escape. Chief goes in with Brendan and me, he's the warrant man, big Ithaca pump in his mitts, spotless white vest. Vestibule door is unlocked. No elevator. Clomp up the stairs, pause on the top landing. Apartment 6-B is left rear, a maroon door with a plastic American flag on it.

As we're catching our collective breaths, we hear voices, the door opens, and out comes a blonde lady with a large mutt on a leash.

"Let's go!" Chief says.

We run down the hall, the dog starts barking, the lady screams, the dog breaks away, comes at us with his teeth bared, leaps directly at me; I kick him in midair, he yelps and goes flying behind us. Lady screams again, runs inside, tries to slam the door, but Brendan's got his foot in it. Here comes the dog again, running like a Greyhound, we jump inside and slam the door a split-second before he leaps and hits it— *wham!* Lady's screaming, running down the hallway. As we chase her into the living room, a guy in pajamas jumps up from a convertible couch. Can't see who it is right away, light's too dim.

Chief crouches, shotgun pointed. "Move, sucker, and you're gone!"

Guy freezes in a kneeling position on the bed. Brendan and I exchange a glance. This is a kid, jet-black hair, can't be more than twenty, twenty-one. Brendan goes to the bedroom, revolver drawn, opens the door. Blonde lady is on the bed crying and a little girl of about nine or ten is trying to comfort her, crying too.

Chief lowers his gun. "Who are you, son?"

"Peter Kenny. Who the fuck are *you?*"

"Police. Don't panic, boy, just relax. Where's Laslo?"

Kid snaps on a lamp, blinks at us. "*Who?*"

"Ron Laslo. We know he's here."

"Ain't nobody here named Laslo! Just my sister, her daughter, me and the dog, that's it! And my sister's got a bad—"

"You saying you don't *know* Ron Laslo?"

Kid jumps off the bed, fully awake now. "Listen, you asshole, I don't *know* anybody named Laslo, I never heard the fuckin' *name* before! And I'll tell you something else: You better get a doctor up here fast, because my sister's got a bad heart!"

He goes in the bedroom. His sister's crying and groaning, holding her chest, the little girl's on the floor now, screaming and crying. Brendan hustles around the rest of the apartment, it's a small one-bedroom deal. Nobody else in the place. Dog's howling, growling, scratching outside the front door, waking the whole building. It's now 6:55. Good morning, America.

Chief grabs the phone, calls Emergency Service, tells them to get an ambulance here fast. Now he gets on his walkie-talkie, orders the raid team back to the cars. Man's got fire in his eyes. Meantime, Peter Kenny's going around with a pencil and paper, getting our shield numbers.

"Brendan!" Chief barks. "Go out and get some brandy for this woman and I don't give a rat's ass how you do it!"

Brendan stands there, face quickly assuming his precinct-famous Hurt Expression. "Beggin' your pardon, sir, but—"

"What?"

"I just—there's a vicious animal outside that door, sir."

"*What?!*"

"Just—I mean, just *listen* to him, sir!"

We listen to a bowel-freezing series of barks, growls, howls, and frantic clawing at the door.

"Beggin' your pardon, sir," Brendan says softly, "but I think that fucker's lookin' to tear me apart."

Peter Kenny to the rescue: "I'll handle the dog, she's never hurt a fly. Come on." Walks calmly down the hall, yelling dog-talk to the door: "Good girl, Daisy, good girl! It's okay, sweetheart!"

Brendan follows at a distance. Considerable distance.

"Rawlings!" Chief says. "I want to see you!"

I follow him into the little bathroom; he closes the door and speaks quietly. "Rawlings, how the fuck could a thing like this *happen!*"

"Don't know, sir."

He puts his shotgun in the corner, sits on the toilet seat, holds his head in his hands. "Almost thirty years on the job and I've never, ever, raided the wrong fuckin' *house.* If the *News* ever gets wind of this—if Vinnie Casandra ever gets hold of this, he'll start another fuckin' *cartoon* series. If the commissioner ever gets wind of it, I'm gone, buddy. *Gone!* How could you guys *do* this to me?!"

I explain how we got the number, how Jessica called New York Telephone Security, waited for the call-back routine, all standard procedure. "Name of the security man who called back is Roberto Sanchez. All I can think, he must've fucked up."

Chief sits back on the toilet now, his whole torso seems to collapse into the big white bulletproof vest. Looks like the underside of an ancient turtle. Makes a low sound in his throat, followed by an ironic, almost hysterical little laugh. "He must've fucked up."

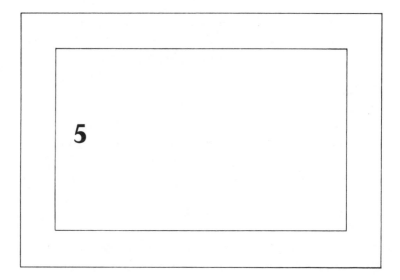

5

TURNS OUT THAT'S EXACTLY what happened. When
we get back to the Twentieth Precinct on West Eighty-second,
Chief goes directly to Marty's office, calls New York Telephone Security himself, speaks to the supervisor of the night
shift (it's now only 7:45 A.M.), leaves a call-back number.
Supervisor calls back instantly, listens to the problem, checks
the computer himself, discovers the number 865-3971 is actually listed to a Mrs. Suzanne Forbes, 315 West 106th Street,
apartment 2-B. He apologizes for Mr. Sanchez's mistake; man
happens to be a new employee in their bilingual group. Chief
hangs up, stares at the phone, talks to it: "Fuckin' Ricans, give
'em a job, try to do the right thing, whaddaya get? Bilingual
illiterates." Now he calls Mat Murphy at home, tells him we
need new warrants with the new address immediately. Mat
says he'll hop a cab down to the Criminal Courts Building,
grab the first judge he can find, deliver the warrants to us
himself as soon as possible. Doesn't even ask what happened.
Knows. Chief's tone says it all.

Mat arrives with the warrants 9:20, off we go, same raid team, four cars, appointment with destiny. Up West End Avenue to 106th, turn left, make a quick pass. Wide, two-way street, brighter and somewhat cleaner than others in the area. Number 315 is on the north side, not far from Riverside. House is one of those old four-story brownstones that was once a fashionable private home. Front is convex, large windows with elaborate black wrought-iron ballustrades. At the top of the stoop, two plain brownstone pillars distinguish this place from most of the others.

We all park on Riverside near 107th. Chief gets on his walkie-talkie, tells Jessica to take a walk, look the house over. Ten minutes later, she's back. Bingo. Our black Mazda RX-7 is parked near the corner of West End; plate checks. House has two apartments to a floor, each appears to be a floor-through. Fire escape in rear. Second-floor windows in front are only about ten feet from the sidewalk. Chief decides to surround it the same way as the one on Ninety-fourth.

Approach the building one by one, front and rear. Chief gives everyone time to get positioned, then Brendan and I accompany him. It's now about 9:50, overcast but fairly bright, pleasant breeze from the river, very few people on the street. Two small girls are drawing pictures in yellow chalk on the front of the adjoining building.

As we reach the top step, we see our reflections in the glass door, partly obscured by large gold numbers: 315. Step into the small foyer, glance at the names over the doorbells. Chief rings the bell for apartment 1-A. Young man in a shirt and tie opens his apartment door, looks through the glass vestibule door. Chief points to the shield on his vest. Young man opens the door quickly, looks at the shotgun with wide eyes.

"Police raid," Chief tells him quietly. "Doesn't concern you. Go back in your apartment, lock the door, don't open it to anybody."

Three of us clomp up the dark stairway to the second floor,

pause on the landing. Brendan and I draw our service revolvers, look around for cover. Chief indicates either side of the door to apartment 2-B. We walk to our positions quietly, flatten ourselves against the wall. Chief flattens himself against the left side of the door, rings the bell. Silence. Footsteps.

Female voice: "Who's there?"

Chief: "Police. We have a warrant for the arrest of Ronald Drake Laslo."

"Wait a minute, I'm not dressed."

"Open up!" Chief shouts.

"Wait a minute!"

"Open up or we'll blow it open!"

Click. She opens the door a crack with the chain still on. Can't see her face, but her voice sounds young. "Ron's not here right now, just my son and myself. I'm Suzanne Forbes. What's this all about?"

"Open anyway," Chief says, still flattened. Holds out the two warrants with his left hand. "We've got a search warrant for the apartment."

Mrs. Forbes removes the chain, opens the door wide, a very attractive but frightened brunette, late twenties, maybe five-seven and 120, blue bathrobe clutched to her neck. We fan out cautiously through the apartment. Her seven-year-old son sits at the breakfast table, wide-eyed. It's a relatively large three-bedroom layout. No Laslo, but we find what looks to be the bedroom he's using. Now we follow the chief into the kitchen, holster our revolvers. Forbes sits at the table next to her son, pushes back her hair, blinks at us in the bright light.

"Where is he?" Chief demands.

"He went out. I don't know."

"Come on, his car's just down the block!"

"Will you tell me what this is all about?"

Chief sits opposite her now, places his shotgun on the floor, tries the quiet approach. "He's wanted for murder, Mrs. Forbes."

"Murder? Ron?"

"Murder, rape, and robbery." He hands her the arrest warrant.

She glances at the warrant, shakes her head. "I can't—I just can't believe it. All I know, he's just gotten a divorce. He asked me if he could stay here for a while."

"Where is he, Mrs. Forbes?"

"He went out maybe ten, fifteen minutes ago to get a haircut."

"Any idea where, which barbershop?"

"Yes, it's a new place, I recommended it—Unisex Hair Salon, at Ninety-sixth and Broadway. He had an appointment for ten-fifteen."

We all glance at our watches: 10:03.

"Did he have a gun with him?" I ask.

"Yes, he always carries it."

Chief uses his walkie-talkie to call the rest of the team inside. Five minutes later we're all in the kitchen, he's telling us his game plan: Jessica, Brendan and I will accompany him to the salon; Marty and Jerry will follow us. The two detectives from the Twentieth will remain in the apartment with a shotgun in case Laslo evades us; one of them will begin a thorough search of the bedroom he's been using. Obviously, Jessica's the least likely to be recognized, so she'll be the warrant person; after we surround the salon, she'll enter alone, check out the logistics while she's making an appointment, then report back to us. If it's not crowded, we'll try to collar him inside. If there's a significant danger to the customers or employees, we'll have to wait until he's through, radio for help, quietly block off the area in front, and take him when he exits. If circumstances make that impossible, we'll wait until he returns to the apartment, take him there.

Off we go in the October chill, two cars this time, north on Riverside to 108th, east to Broadway, south to Ninety-sixth. Unisex Hair Salon is situated on the southeast corner, entrance on Broadway, a recently renovated five-story building. Salon itself occupies the ground floor, modern exterior, big plant-filled windows, large chrome and glass door. Brendan double-parks the chief's car on Broadway, about three doors south of the salon; Jerry double-parks Marty's car on Ninety-sixth just off Broadway with a good view of the entrance.

Chief turns, looks at Jessica in back, seated to my left. "Now, Jessica, I don't have to remind you, this guy is armed. Armed and dangerous."

"Yes, sir."

Checks his watch. "Ten-fourteen. Unless they're running late, he should be in the chair now. Think you can recognize him from the back?"

"I think so, yes. And there are mirrors, of course."

"All right. Now, I've been thinking on the way down here. I want to give you an option, Jessica. Instead of just going in, making an appointment, finding out where he's at, I think you should use your own good discretion here. You got the experience, you been in situations like this before."

"Yes, I have."

Chief nods, glances at me, then narrows his eyes at her. "All right. Soon's you go in, I'm sending Rawlings here to cover the front. It's a glass door, he'll be able to see what's what in there. Now, if the logistics are right, Jessica, if he's far enough away from the others, go ahead and use your discretion. If you think you can go ahead and collar this guy on the spot—safely, quietly—just give Rawlings a signal. Soon's you make your move, in he comes to back you up. At which time we'll all be out of the cars and ready to move inside."

She turns to me, moves her left hand to her hair. "I'll stand sideways, push back my hair with my left hand."

"Okay," I tell her.

"If he's too close to other people," she says, "I'll simply make the appointment and leave."

"In that case," Chief says, "we'll block off the immediate

area very gradually and plan to take him when he comes out. Brendan, I want you on the back door of this place. Head south on Broadway. If you can't find an alley close by, go in one of the stores, show your gold, go through fast. Take your walkie-talkie, tell us when you're set. Code names—you're Haircut One, we're Two, Marty's Three. Get going, we'll wait."

Brendan jumps out, heads south. Chief gets on the walkie-talkie now, briefs Marty and Jerry, code names, the whole shot. Man's always loved code names. Me, I think they suck. What can I tell you?

About three minutes later, Brendan's voice comes over, heavy with static: "Haircut One to Haircut Two, over."

"Haircut Two," Chief says.

"Ready at the back door, over."

"Ten-four."

Jessica transfers her service revolver from her purse to the right-hand pocket of her blue windbreaker. Chief hands her the arrest warrant, she folds it in half, tucks it in her left-hand pocket. I'm on the sidewalk side, so I open the door, step out, give her a hand. Not many pedestrians this time of morning, but traffic's fairly heavy. I wait by the car as she walks directly to the entrance. Cuts a nice figure in designer jeans and boots. Opens the glass door, goes inside. Now I walk leisurely toward the entrance, stop in front of the window to the right, look through the plants. She's standing at the counter in the crowded little waiting area, talking with the receptionist, making an appointment. Now the kid's writing it down in her book, Jessica's glancing around the back room. From my angle, I can see maybe six hairdressers working along the left side, three along the back, ample space between all of them; I can't see the right side.

Jessica pushes her hair back with her left hand, then waves to an imaginary friend who's having her hair done, and walks casually into the back room. Boom, I'm in that door in three seconds, holster unsnapped, adrenaline pumping.

I see her stop behind the fourth chair to the left, right hand in her jacket pocket. As she moves in close and says something, Laslo whirls his chair around in a blur, knocks her sprawling toward the next chair. I draw my revolver, drop to a combat crouch, but now everybody's screaming, a wall of men and women are running from the room, straight toward me, I'm bumped and shoved, I point my gun toward the ceiling, I got no choice, I can't see Jessica or Laslo for at least four or five seconds. Now I see them. He's behind her, facing me, he's got her in a choke-hold with his left arm, and he's got his gun against the back of her head. He's yelling something at her, but I can't hear over all the screaming. Jessica reaches into her jacket pocket very slowly, removes her gun by the handle with her fingertips, holds it out to the side, drops it.

I'm still in the crouch, gun pointed at them. *"Give it up, Laslo, you're surrounded!"*

He tightens his choke-hold on her. *"Listen,* you fuckin' asshole, I'm only gonna say this once! Drop your weapon right now or I'll blow her fuckin' brains all over this room! I got nothin' to *lose!* I'm a dead man *anyway!"*

Chief's voice booms from the waiting room: "Laslo, you're surrounded! There's no way out!"

"Vadney? he shouts. "That you, Vadney?"

"Yeah, it's me, and we got—"

"Shut up, you fuckin' scumbag! *Listen* for once in your life! Listen *hard!* This kid's *life* depends on it! Here's what's goin' down: I'm walkin' out of here with my gun flat against this kid's head! The gun's *cocked,* Vadney, you *got* that? *Cocked!* The slightest move to stop me, she's dead! We're walkin' out of here, Vadney, and you're comin' *with* us! We're gonna walk straight to your car! *You're* gonna drive us out of here! You *got* that?"

By now the screaming's all over, everybody's out on the sidewalk. I don't turn, I don't move a muscle, but I know

Vadney's in a combat crouch, probably with a shotgun, and I suspect Marty and Jerry are also inside by now, both with shotguns, right behind him. Jessica's face is red in the strong choke-hold and both her hands are gripping Laslo's left forearm, pulling instinctively, trying to prevent the pressure from getting worse.

Chief breaks the short silence, voice calm and low: "Rawlings, drop it, stand aside." He places his shotgun on the floor, click-clunk. "Marty, Jerry, put 'em down, stand aside."

Laslo waits. Then: "Now, the three of you, kick the shotguns away from you. You, kick the revolver away."

In the silence guns make scraping sounds as they slide across the linolium.

"Where you parked?" Laslo asks.

Nobody answers.

"Vadney! Where the fuck you *parked?"*

"About three doors south."

"All right, I want an escort through that fuckin' crowd to the car. Vadney, walk toward me. Slow."

Chief's leather heels click slowly. He passes me, face sweating, head up.

"Stop right there," Laslo says, softer now. "Turn around slow. Okay. Now, real slow, reach back, use your fingertips, ease the weapon from the holster. That's it. Nice and easy. Now drop it."

Chief bends at the knees to allow a shorter drop.

"Now kick it way off to the side."

He winces, listening to the nickel-plated .38 scrape along.

"Okay, you two clowns by the door. Same thing. Turn, face the door, reach back slow, use just the fingertips. Real slow. That's the stuff. Now drop 'em. Now, same thing, kick 'em aside. All right." He nods at me. "You, you walk over to the other two. Slow. Stand between 'em."

As I turn and walk toward them, I can see the crowd gathering outside. Probably twenty-five, thirty people already, so I'm sure we'll have a squad car along soon. I stand between Marty and Jerry.

"Okay," Laslo says. "Now, all four of you guys, nice and slow, reach just below your knees and lift your pant legs. That's it. Way up."

He's looking for an ankle holster, of course, and he finds one on Marty. Big and black, right ankle.

"Ease it out, asshole. Fingertips."

Marty unsnaps the hammer strap, pulls the .38 out by the handle, tosses it off to the side.

"All right, the three of you, get your handcuffs out, place 'em on the floor to your left."

As we do, I see two uniformed cops push their way through the crowd and head for the front door fast. A hairdresser in a green smock stops the first officer, speaks to him, points inside. He squints in, sees us clearly. He's just a kid, maybe early twenties.

"You in the middle," Laslo snaps. "Cuff the guy on your left first, use his cuffs. Let me hear 'em click tight. Behind his back."

I cuff Marty as loosely as I can.

"Now the other one. Use his cuffs. Let's hear 'em click up tight."

As I cuff Jerry, I glance out at the two officers. The young one is pushing back the crowd as quickly as he can. The older one is speaking into his walkie-talkie. I'm thinking about Brendan at the back door. I'm wondering if that door is locked.

"Okay, Vadney, walk straight ahead. Cuff the middle guy, use his cuffs. Move it."

Chief clicks toward me, bends to pick up my cuffs, slaps them on fast and tight.

"Okay, stay right where you are." He lowers his voice to Jessica: "Now listen, baby, and listen good. I'm gonna loosen up just enough so you can walk. This thing's cocked, that's no bullshit. You try anything—elbows, legs, a karate shot, *any* thing—your fuckin' skull gets blown away. Me, I don't give a fuck one way or the other, I'm dead, I got nothin' to lose. It's your choice. All right, move it."

We hear them shuffle toward us, Jessica's throat making painful strangled sounds. Outside, the crowd's away from the front now. I can't see either of the cops, so I assume they've taken cover, waiting for help. The shuffling stops. Jessica and Laslo are directly behind the chief, who's directly behind me.

"We're going' out in this formation. Slowly. One wrong move, she's dead, then I turn it on myself. Vadney, I'm sure you got cops out there, so you better give 'em orders soon's the door opens. And I mean orders, loud and clear: 'This is Chief Vadney! Hold your fire! Police officer hostage!' Then we walk to the car, you in front, us in back. Straight up Broadway till I tell you different. You *got* that?"

"I got it."

"Okay. You, the little guy in the middle: When we reach the door, you kick it open slowly. You, on the right there: Hold it open with your shoulder. We all stop at that point. Then Vadney says his piece. Any questions?"

"Yeah," I tell him softly. "The young lady sounds like she's strangling. Until you let up on her, I don't move."

Jessica's painful sounds continue for a few seconds, then ease up considerably. When she catches her breath, she whispers: "Okay. I'm okay."

I nod. "Let's go."

We move ahead. I place my foot against the glass door, push it open slowly, Jerry holds it open with his shoulder. I can see the two cops flattened against the wall on either side of the door, weapons drawn, pointing up. The crowd is backed up about twenty yards on the sidewalk, left and right, and the noise level increases when they see us.

Vadney's voice is calm but loud: "Hold your fire! Hold your fire! This is Chief Vadney! A police officer is being held at gunpoint! Give us safe passage! Do *not* attempt to interfere! That is an order!"

"Move out!" Laslo says.

We walk into the sunlight in our three-one-two formation and head south toward the car. When the crowd spots Laslo holding Jessica with the gun to her head, they scatter fast. Cars and trucks pull over and stop to gawk. Chief's car is double-parked, so Marty, Jerry, and I step off the curb, walk to the side of the car, and stand there.

"Vadney, drive!" Laslo orders. "Open both doors."

Chief walks to the driver's side, they follow close behind. He opens the back door first, then the front, and climbs inside. Laslo shoves Jessica in back, jumps in beside her, keeps the gun pointed at her head as he reaches back and slams the door.

"Take off!" he orders.

Chief pulls out into snarled traffic, blasts his horn, snakes around three or four vehicles, and speeds away. Whole thing happens so fast it's difficult to believe. Marty, Jerry, and I stand there in the cool October sun, hands cuffed behind our backs, and watch Vadney's dark blue 1983 Ford Fairmont disappear into the Broadway traffic.

6

FORTY-FIVE MINUTES LATER, while virtually every cop in the city is concentrating on the tri-state high-priority APB, a uniformed officer from the Twenty-fifth Precinct, who hasn't heard the APB, is writing a routine ticket behind a double-parked vehicle near the corner of 125th Street and Lenox Avenue in Harlem, when he thinks he hears shouts from inside the car. Traffic noises are loud at that intersection, so he's not sure. When he looks in the closed windows, he sees a man on the back seat in a contorted position, wrists and ankles cuffed together behind his back, hog-tie style. The man's shouting for help, but can't be heard very well because of the closed windows. Policeman tries to open the doors, but they're locked. Now he uses his walkie-talkie to call a squad car in the vicinity. When he describes the vehicle as a dark-blue late-model Ford Fairmont, exactly four squad cars squeal recklessly to the scene, arrive within seconds of each other, sirens screaming.

Chief is rushed to the Twenty-fifth Precinct, 120 East 119th

Street (has to be carried in, of course, to his mortification), where the cuffs are laboriously cut off. Rumor has it, he's more than humiliated, he's mad now, really hot, which is rare for him. Says he wants Laslo for himself, he wants his ass, he wants the fucker dead. Now he calls Mat Murphy at headquarters, tells him to set up a meeting in his office fast, 12:30 this afternoon. He wants just Grady, Pearson, Marty, Brendan and me. Reason he wants Grady there is transparent. Press on this latest development could be downright embarrassing to the department; he's out to minimize that damage. My guess, Grady will have a first-draft press release by meeting time, dictated by Vadney, in an attempt to head 'em off at the pass, particularly the *News,* where venomous Vinnie Casandra will be looking to bust chops.

When we file in at 12:30 sharp, there are six NYPD-blue Duo-Tang presentation folders at our places around the conference table, next to six legal-sized yellow pads and sharpened pencils. Ever-present silver Sony TCM-600 Cassette-Corder occupies the center of the table. Chief's on the phone with Commissioner Reilly, listening mostly, brows knitted, shirtsleeves rolled to the elbow, wrists red, tie yanked way down, collar open wide enough to show the ring borne of hog-tied frustration. One glance at his ass-chewed expression and you capture the carefree aura of what's to come.

Grady tells us to go ahead and read the release. Naturally, it's typed flawlessly on his IBM Correcting Selectric III, and exhibits include 8″-×-10″ black-and-white glossies of the drama's known protagonists: Laslo looks devilishly constipated; Chief looks devilishly swashbuckling, which may be a mixed metaphor, but so is Vadney.

POLICE DEPARTMENT
NEW YORK, N. Y. 10013

CONTACT: DET. JERRY GRADY   FOR IMMEDIATE RELEASE

PRESS RELATIONS

(212) 477-9777

CHIEF VADNEY RESCUES HOSTAGE

NEW YORK, October 19—Chief of Detectives Walter
Vadney, 53, rescued a young female undercover detective
who was taken hostage at gunpoint this morning by a
suspected murderer and mass-rapist, when a covert
operation to arrest the man failed.

According to police, the undercover detective entered
the Unisex Hair Salon, Broadway at 96th St., Manhattan,
at 10:15 a.m., where the suspect, identified as
Ronald Drake Laslo, 36, of New York, was having a
haircut.

Acting alone but backed up by Vadney and other
officers who had the building surrounded, the
undercover detective attempted to arrest Laslo without
endangering other customers, but was knocked to the
floor and overpowered, police said. The salon was
quickly evacuated.

Armed with shotguns, Vadney and three other detectives

immediately entered the building but were thwarted by
Laslo, who held the young woman at gunpoint and
repeatedly threatened to kill her, police said. Vadney
had no choice but to order his men to drop their
weapons.

After handcuffing the three detectives, police said,
the suspect forced Vadney to alert officers outside the
building to the hostage situation and order them not to
interfere because of the serious risk to the woman.

According to police, Laslo then escaped, forcing
Vadney to drive an unmarked police car, while he
continued to hold a gun to the woman's head in the back
seat.

Shortly afterward, police reported, while driving at a
high rate of speed, Vadney suddenly hit the brakes,
spinning the vehicle around and throwing Laslo against
the seat. A fistfight followed, during which Vadney
disarmed the suspect. Cut and bleeding profusely, Laslo
ran from the car into a crowded street. Vadney elected
not to give chase because of the potential danger to
pedestrians.

This afternoon the suspect is still at large and
police have initiated a three-state manhunt. In
addition, because of the attempted kidnapping, the FBI
announced that it had officially entered the case and
will start its own investigation in concert with local
and state police.

Frankly, all I can say, it's difficult to keep a straight face. As
the chief winds up his conversation with Reilly, I glance across

the table at Grady, give him a raised eyebrow. He shrugs, rolls his eyes. Marty and Pearson are rereading certain paragraphs with concerned expressions. Brendan looks like he just dropped one.

Chief finally finishes with Reilly, hangs up, narrows his eyes as he surveys our faces. He gets up with an effort, legs obviously very stiff from the ordeal, rubs his wrists, leans across the table to his Sony, presses the red record button. We're on.

"Comments, questions, suggestions?" he asks.

Pearson frowns, clears his throat. "The first paragraph and the next-to-last paragraph. I'd like clarification."

Chief sits down now, opens his folder, reads the paragraphs slowly, as if for the first time. "Yeah, Dave, what about them?"

"I heard a—I just heard a different version, that's all."

"Different version? Who from?"

"Lieutenant Holland. John Holland up at the Twenty-fifth."

Chief nods. "When?"

"When?" Pearson glances at his watch. "I'd say around—eleven-fifteen. He called to tell me you were safe. At the time, they were—he told me that his men were—well, cutting the cuffs off you."

Chief gazes at him in silence for a moment. Then: "That was before I ordered the entire incident up there classified. At this point, it's strictly classified intelligence. Any officer of any rank up there—or anywhere else in the department—who discusses the incident with anybody—*any*body—is subject to immediate suspension without pay and possible dismissal from the department. That includes everyone in this room. Do I make myself clear?"

Marty nods, speaks quietly. "Chief, I'm not quite certain I understand your rationale on this."

"Rationale?"

"Yes, sir. The truth is, Laslo's holding Jessica hostage and he'll use her as an extremely valuable bargaining tool. My guess is, he'll contact us soon and make demands. He'll probably want safe passage out of the country, plus a lot of cash, in return for her life. So what possible good is a press release that distorts these facts?"

"Good question, Marty, glad you asked." Chief sits forward, clasps his fingers together on the table, stares at his bruised wrists. "I will not, under any circumstances whatsoever, permit this department to be intimidated, embarrassed, or subjected to possible ridicule in the press because of this mentally deranged ex-cop. He's already disgraced the department and damaged the morale of every honest cop we have, which is to say the overwhelming majority of our people. His days of hurting this department are over. Finished. Like I told all the people at the Twenty-fifth—I called a meeting of all of 'em before I left. I ordered the incident classified, of course, and then I said: 'Ladies and gentlemen, here's the bottom line. If we stick together on this, if we keep this hostage incident classified, we're returning to the department something that a minority of degenerates like Laslo steal from each and every one of us: Dignity. That's right. Dignity. Dignity in the eyes of the press, which translates into dignity in the eyes of the public that we serve. We deserve it. We've earned it. We refuse to have it taken away from us by perverts like Laslo.' That's what I told 'em up there. That's what I'm telling you. That's the way I feel."

"Chief," I say softly. "May I make just one observation?"

"Sure."

"I'm not an expert in hostage situations, far from it, but I'm just wondering. By not telling our own people that Jessica's a hostage, we may be inadvertently placing her at unnecessary risk."

"Be specific, Rawlings."

"Well, sir, if our own people—local, state, federal—think Laslo's out there alone, and if they corner him someplace, there's at least some probability you'll have a shootout, in my judgment."

Chief thinks on it. "Which brings up another point. Spread the word on this. From here on out, Laslo's *mine*. I don't want any trigger-happy cowboys trying to drop this fucker on their own. Understood? Rawlings, you hear me?"

"Loud and clear."

"Chief," Pearson says, "this last paragraph here confirms the FBI's starting its own investigation. How you intend to handle them?"

"Just like always, Dave. Tell 'em nothing. Give 'em nothing. Just what's in the release." He sits back, speaks quietly now. "I'm personally gonna collar this fucker, dead or alive. Sooner or later, he's gonna make a mistake. I know it, he knows it, we all know it. He's gonna have to make his move fast. He's got no car, he's got no money except what he had on him, he's got nobody left to turn to, not even relatives. All he's got, as far as we know, are the clothes on his back and one service revolver. Period. His picture and description have been in every newspaper in this city and on every local TV news show. When this new thing hits the media, attempted kidnapping of police officers, combined with the three-state APB, somebody's gonna spot him. Somebody, somewhere. He can't stay holed up forever. Okay, now, here's what's happening. I got a news conference scheduled for one-thirty this afternoon. Here's what I want you people to do. First off, go back to your offices, get the word out to every single solitary informant in your areas that we want this guy real bad. Hold out the carrots. Any scrap of information they got—*any*thing —follow it up. Mat Murphy's on the phone right now speaking with every commanding officer in every precinct, telling 'em the same thing. *Every* informant, salaried or otherwise, we want this fucker and money's no object. That's it for now. Comments, questions, suggestions?"

Brendan glances around, waiting for the others, straightens his tie, clears his throat. Must say he looks sharp now, blue blazer, white shirt, dark tie, gray trousers. Acting on my advice, he's kept that outfit in his locker since he was named to the special-assignment team, specifically for the purpose of our meetings with the chief. Of course, I do the same thing, but I've had the dubious distinction of working around the chief longer than he has. Chief's philosophy about appearance happens to be quite specific. Quotes George Steinbrenner: "No man on my ballclub is allowed to dress as bad as he plays." Words to that effect. Anyhow, Brendan sees nobody else has anything to say, he sits forward, speaks quietly, realizing his words are destined to be filed for eternity:

"Beggin' your pardon, sir."

"Yeah, Brendan."

"You mentioned relatives a while back."

"Yeah."

"Well, sir, as you know, we hit somethin' of a blank wall on his relatives so far. We could only find his wife at first, and now his cousin this morning."

"Yeah."

"Well, sir, I happened on somethin' the other day, I think it might be worth checkin' out. I was in Hal Kendig's the other night and we were talkin'—"

"Where?"

"Hal Kendig's, sir, Hal Kendig's Speak Easy Saloon, just up the street from the Nineteenth."

Chief glances at his watch. "Brendan, get to the point, huh? I got a tight schedule here."

"Yes, sir. The thing of it is, sir, I was talkin' to Hal Kendig. See, Hal and me, we both happen to be jazz buffs from way back, we go to various jazz clubs around—"

"For Christ's sake, man, will you get to the fuckin' *point!*"

"Sorry, sir. The point is, I think I might have a lead on Laslo's father. I think I know who he is and where he is. And his mother, too."

"I thought we came up empty on them."

"We did, sir. Apparently, we were checkin' under the wrong names. They go by his father's stage name: Bobby Kane. Y'know, the jazz drummer?"

Chief frowns, sits up now. "Are you—? Bobby *Kane?*"

"Yes, sir, according to Hal Kendig."

"Well, I'll be a son of a bitch."

"Yes, sir. Of course, I'm not completely—"

"Wait a minute now, hold on a minute. I mean, I don't know all that much about jazz, but even *I* know *that* name."

"Yes, sir, he's one of the most famous jazz drummers, he played with Dorsey in the forties and Harry James in the sixties. He's got his own band now, his own club; a lot of the experts put him in the same league with Buddy Rich and Gene Krupa."

"How come nobody knew about this?"

Brendan clears his throat. "As I understand it, sir, on his application, on Laslo's original application, he listed his father as 'Robert A. Laslo,' which is still the man's legal name, he never changed it. And he listed his father's occupation as 'musician.' That's all we had to go on."

"Excellent work, Brendan. We might be on to something here. You and Rawlings drop everything, go check this guy out. Maybe we got a break, finally, it's about time. If this guy's actually his father, Laslo might very well hit on him for some money. He's desperate enough. Money, hell, Laslo might be holding Jessica there. Where's he live?"

"I don't know that yet, sir, I haven't had—"

"Find out fast. Where's the jazz club?"

"West Thirty-third, near the Garden."

"Get goin'. Report directly to me."

First things first, we check the Manhattan telephone directory. No listing for Bobby Kane or Robert A. Kane. Doesn't surprise us. Check the telephone books for the other four boroughs, just to be on the safe side. Nothing. Next we call New York Telephone Security, ask for our bilingual buddy Roberto Sanchez, figure we'll give him a chance to redeem himself. Sanchez goes through the callback routine. We ask him for the unlisted number and address for Bobby Kane or

Robert A. Kane. Punches it up on the computer very, very carefully: Bobby Kane, 10 West Sixty-sixth Street, apartment 34-B, number 362-1547. Thank him kindly. Of course, we have absolutely no intention of calling Kane or going up there cold. Just want the information for later.

Although it's only 1:15 in the afternoon (seems like a very long day already), we decide to drive up to the jazz club, called Bobby's Drum, 139 West Thirty-third, across from the Statler Hilton Hotel, in the Madison Square Garden area. We know it's closed, but we want to look around. Place turns out to be downstairs from a restaurant called Downbeat. Enter through heavy glass doors into a foyer with glass walls. Above the carpeted stairway down to the club is an aluminium-framed color blowup of Bobby Kane in action; alongside are smaller photos of Nipsy Russell and Carmen McRae, who are appearing as guest stars. A second set of glass doors, to the right, open to a carpeted hallway leading to the restaurant, with a bar area just outside. Whole atmosphere spells class.

We go through the bar area and into the restaurant, discreetly show our gold to the tuxedoed maître d', ask to see the manager. He comes out quickly, a tall, heavyset man, graying at the temples, wearing a dark pinstriped three-piece.

"Gentlemen, I'm Carl Jenkins. What can I do for you?"

Brendan shows his gold again. "I'm Detective Thomas, this is Detective Rawlings. Just like to ask you a few routine questions."

"Certainly, right this way." Leads us back through the bar area, selects a table away from guests. "May I offer you anything?"

"No, thanks," Brendan says. "This'll only take a few minutes. We want to get in touch with Bobby Kane, this afternoon if possible. Do you know the name of his agent or manager?"

"His manager, yes. Max Alexander. He dines here frequently."

Brendan jots the name down. "Would you have his office address or phone number?"

"Yes, he has an account with us." Jenkins motions to one of the waiters, who comes over quickly. "Angelo, will you bring me the telephone, please?" Then, to us: "I just want to call my secretary. May I ask, is Mr. Kane in any trouble?"

"None at all," I tell him. "Just want to ask some questions."

Angelo comes back with a white telephone, places it in front of Jenkins, carries the cord to a wall outlet nearby, plugs it in. Jenkins dials his secretary, asks for the address and phone number, repeats them aloud for Brendan, who jots them down: 175 Riverside Drive, apartment 17-D; 877-1355.

"Thank you, Mr. Jenkins," Brendan says. "We appreciate your cooperation."

"Glad to oblige."

"May we use your phone in private?" I ask.

"Certainly." He stands, shakes our hands. "When you finish, just leave the phone on the table. Good afternoon."

"Good afternoon." Brendan pushes the phone toward me. "You got a better telephone style. Real eloquence."

"Watch your language, you're in a class joint." I glance at the number, dial. Rings four times.

"Hello."

"May I speak to Max Alexander?"

"Speaking."

"Mr. Alexander, this is Detective John Rawlings from the Nineteenth Precinct."

"Yeah."

"I understand you're Bobby Kane's manager, is that correct?"

"Right. What's the trouble?"

"No trouble, we'd just like to arrange a meeting with him, if possible, and ask a few questions."

"Is this about Ron?"

"Yes, it is."

"Maybe I can save you some time and effort. Bobby don't know where he is. He hasn't heard nothing from him for months now."

"I see. Would he be willing to talk with us anyway?"

Max hesitates. "He might. I could try. I mean, he's always cooperated with the police, his whole career, he's always made a point of it. See, Bobby wants the kid caught, that's the thing. Y'know, before he kills somebody else. He keeps talking about how the kid is sick, how he needs help. Tell you what. It's—almost two o'clock now, so he'd be up by now. See, he don't get to bed till about four. I'll give him a call, see how he feels about it. We're having lunch at three o'clock up at DiLillo's on West Fifty-third. Maybe you could stop by, have a cup of coffee, ask your questions, get it over with."

"Sounds good to me."

"Okay, look, I'll call him now and call you back. You're at the Nineteenth Precinct?"

"No, we're at the Downbeat."

"Oh. You in the bar there?"

"Right."

"Okay, look, sit still, I'll call him, call you right back. Now, tell me your name again, I'm sorry."

"Detective John Rawlings."

"Okay, John, I'll get back to you in—say, five minutes."

"I'll be here."

Brendan goes up to the bar, orders a couple of beers, tells the bartender we're expecting a call within five minutes. Bartender says our phone is the same number as the bar's, just pick it up at our table. We sit back, have a cigar with our beer, enjoy the elegant ambience. Six, seven minutes later, phone rings softly, I take it.

"Hello."

"John?"

"Right, Max."

"Bobby says he's more than willing to cooperate in any way he can. He wants you to join us for lunch."

"Appreciate it, Max. Haven't had lunch yet, either."

"Okay, three o'clock, DiLillo's. Know where it is?"

"Sure do."

"We got a table reserved upstairs under Bobby's name. You got a partner with you?"

"Yeah."

"Okay. Just one thing, John. Hope you don't take this the wrong way, but Bobby wants his attorney there. Don't ask me why, he just does. That okay with you?"

"Absolutely."

"See you at three."

7

W E H A V E A W I N D O W T A B L E in the upstairs dining
room at DiLillo's on Fifty-third between Fifth and Sixth.
Popular Italian joint, but it's not crowded now at 3:30. Bobby
Kane's a half-hour late. Max Alexander keeps glancing at his
watch and drumming his knife on the tablecloth, a lean, wiry
guy in his late fifties with short gray-white hair and expensive
sports clothes. Bobby's attorney, Cal Bovallo, adjusts his
glasses as he reads *Newsweek,* thick dark hair white at the
temples, slightly overweight, banker's-gray suit, looks to be in
his early fifties, a guy who smiles a lot. At this point, Brendan
and me are out of small-talk, so we sip our Beefeater martinis,
look down at the crowded sidewalk, garbage cans overflowing
at the curbs, cars and taxis and trucks jammed four-abreast,
bumper-to-bumper, horns blowing, the usual. I'm not hungry
any more, but I'm looking forward to meeting this guy Kane,
Brendan's filled me in on his long career. Started with his
parents in a vaudeville act when he was eighteen months old;
now, at age sixty-six, he's been a drummer for sixty-five years,
and apparently still going strong.

Max checks his watch again. "Something must've happened."

Cal looks up from his magazine. "There's a very simple explanation," he tells Max. "Very simple. Some poor bastard looked crooked at Bobby on the street and got his head busted. A karate shot to the temple. Very clean. Very fast. Like those boards he breaks. He's now being booked for manslaughter. Our defense? Insanity. Not temporary insanity. Permanent, total, congenital, out-and-out bananas insanity."

Max smiles, but he's just not in the mood for that. "No, see, that's the thing about B. He's never late. I mean, you know that. All right, he worked last night, he probably didn't get to bed till four or five. But that don't mean nothing with him. I mean, I've known the man for thirty-five years. He's never late."

Cal tosses the copy of *Newsweek* on the table, open to an article about the New York Jazz Festival.

"Is that a picture of Bobby?" I ask.

He nods. "With Lionel Hampton. Bobby's group really walked away with it."

"The whole festival was dynamite," Max tells me. "Blues, ragtime, Dixieland, swing, bop, pop, jam, they had it all. Dizzy—you hear the number Dizzy pulled? They were interviewing him, some newspaper guys, I don't know. One young cat, he comes up to him, he says, 'Mr. Gillespie, how would you define bop?' Well, Dizzy, he gives him a look, y'know? Says, 'Bop. Bop. How would I define bop?' He thinks about it, he's frowning, holding his forehead, the whole number. Now he straightens up, he clears his throat, they got their pencils and pads all ready, right? He says, 'Well, actually, what it is,' he says, 'I mean, what it *was*—well, see, we just stole some tunes.' "

We all laugh. Max has the accent down cold.

" 'We just stole some tunes,' " he says, laughing, savoring it.

Short time later, when Bobby finally arrives, he walks toward us at a fast clip, staring straight ahead, and it's obvious by his face and posture that he's very angry. Doesn't look sixty-six, nowhere near it, full head of dark hair, modern aviator-style glasses, body lean and hard and almost athletic in a tight white turtleneck and jeans, but his face has mileage.

Max introduces Brendan and me, we shake hands, he says hello to Cal, yanks out his chair, and it starts.

"What happened?" Max asks.

Bobby sits down, leans forward stiffly, clenches his hands on the table, stares at them. Takes a couple of deep breaths.

"What, somebody downstairs?" Max asks.

"The fuckin' *cabbie,*" he says, trying to keep his voice low. "He shouldn't be *driving* a cab, he shouldn't be *allowed* in a cab!"

"What'd he do?" Cal asks.

"Three-fifteen in the afternoon and he can't change a twenty dollar bill! Can't change a *twenty!* I have to get out, I have to go in to the cashier in the *restaurant*—and then *he* gives me an argument!"

"Oh, man," Max says.

Light bulb directly above Bobby's head starts to flicker. It may have been doing that before he arrived, but I didn't notice.

Bobby glances up at it, then concentrates on his hands again. "The fare is two dollars and thirty cents. I go in, I get change, I come out, I give him exactly two dollars and thirty cents. Period. So he tries to do a number on me. I told him exactly what to do. I gave him very specific instructions about what to do."

In the pause, we can hear soft music and the voice of a radio disk jockey. Bobby stares at his hands. Light bulb above his head goes completely out, then flickers on again.

Bobby looks up at it, then at Max. "If somebody doesn't fix that fuckin' thing right *now,* I'm walking out of here."

Max stands up quickly and leaves the table.

"The start of another sunny day," Cal says softly.

Bobby's face reacts first, eyes and mouth closing tightly, as if in pain, then his shoulders are shaking and he's laughing through his nose, and in another few seconds his head's down on the table and his whole body's shaking with laughter. Brendan and I start laughing too, more in relief than anything else. Bobby tries several times to say something to Cal, he can't get it out, they're really howling now. Don't think I've ever seen a man change moods so quickly from one extreme to another.

Max comes back with a short man who's carrying a stepladder. For some reason, just seeing them together breaks Bobby and Cal up again. Max accepts the whole change of mood as if it's an everyday occurrence. He makes the transition immediately, imitates a vaudeville MC, introduces the short man as "Ladders LaRue," and announces he'll now do his act for us: "Screwin' light bulbs." Bobby and Cal applaud. Short man stands there holding his ladder, he doesn't know to whistle or shit. Now Max puts his arm around him, all apologies, and the little guy changes the light bulb in record time.

Before lunch arrives, the radio music changes to a news broadcast. We don't pay much attention to it until somebody hears the name "Higgins," then Bobby wants to listen. Story's about Kenny Higgins, lead singer of the Wild Strawberries, a hot new American rock group. This week, Higgins's latest scuffle with the press happens in Australia on a concert tour and each episode is widely publicized, of course, this clown makes better copy than John McEnroe. First, Higgins's bodyguards rough up some photographers. Next, he announces from the stage in Melbourne that reporters are "bums" and refers to newswomen as "hookers." Next day or so, Australia's in a national uproar. Outraged musicians, stagehands, and other union members rush to the support of the Australian Journalists' Association. Higgins and his group are refused all kinds of services, including fuel for their private jet. One concert has to be cancelled. President of the Australian Council of Trade Unions says flatly, "He'll never get out of

the country until he apologizes." Finally, a joint statement is
released, saying that Higgins meant no moral reflection on
Australian journalists, but reserves the right to criticize in-
dividuals. There's no apology for anything. Embargo's lifted,
tour continues. As the world turns. Newscaster turns to another subject.

Bobby claps his hands, looks happy. "Apologize! Oh, yeah,
that'll be the day. That'll be *the* day when Kenny apologizes
to *those* assholes."

"Tell 'em about *your* tour," Cal says smiling.

Bobby nods, clears his throat once, takes a deep breath with
his teeth clenched, looks at Brendan and me. "This'll give you
an idea of the mentality of these people Kenny's dealing with
down there. I took the big band on a concert tour of Australia
in nineteen sixty-seven. We were in Tasmania for one day, we
did a television show, we were leaving for Melbourne next
morning. So we had this suite in the hotel. Ned and I had a
twin-bedded room and Ron—"

"Ned's his secretary," Max tells us.

"Right, and Ron was with us, he had his own room. Ron
was twenty that year, he'd just gotten out of the Army. He'd
spent three years in the Army, he'd served in Vietnam, so this
was a vacation for him. Okay, we turned in, we were all asleep.
I don't know what time it was, two, three o'clock in the
morning, we heard this loud knocking at the front door.
Y'know, nothing timid—very, very authoritative. Bam-bam-
bam-bam-bam! Ned jumped out of bed; I just opened my eyes.
Next thing, I hear Ned rapping with somebody about something, and I called out, 'What is it?' He said, 'Please come out,
Bobby.' So I did. I put on a robe, a terrycloth robe that the
hotel supplied, I went out into the living room, and a couple
of these cats are already in the room. Cops, plainclothes cops.
Then about nine other cops walked in, all plainclothes cops.
That's no exaggeration. There were actually eleven of these
cats." He glances at Cal. "Right?"

"Correct. It's in the sworn statement."

Bobby lights a cigarette. "It seems so completely outrageous to think about it, even now. So, they come in. And they're just walking around aimlessly; it was a very big suite, the presidential suite. *Aimlessly.* So I said to the sergeant, 'What's happening, what do you want here?' He says, 'We got a search warrant here for narcotics.' I said, 'Oh, yeah? You got a search warrant?' I said, 'Ned, get my glasses.' Got my glasses. So I go to take the warrant, he pulls it back, like so. 'Don't touch it.' All right, okay. So I read it with him holding it. Says they're looking for *heroin.* So I laughed at the cat. And he was—to begin with, he's a real Keystone Cop, y'know? The whole number, he's making a big bust, *The French Connection.* So I said, 'Listen, this is totally ridiculous, man. You won't find any heroin here.' He goes, 'Yeah? We have a search warrant, we'll have a look.' So they start looking. They're all over the place. They're going down the sides of the beds, the pillowcases, lifting up the sheets, lifting up the mattresses, going over the curtains, running the seams of the curtains. One cat went so far—he's looking into the vents of the air conditioners. I mean, it was just unbelievable. I'm standing there, I'm looking at them. Three o'clock in the morning. So I said to the sergeant, I said, 'Listen, while you're tearing the place apart, can I order some breakfast?' He says, 'Yeah.' Real tough cat. So I ordered some scrambled eggs. I'm sitting at the table, eating the scrambled eggs, and there's this cop, a young blond cat, he's sitting next to me, closer than Max is now, and he's staring at me while I'm trying to eat. While all these other maniacs are running all over the place, he's sitting there, staring at me. Never takes his eyes off me. So, finally, I dropped my fork, I looked at the cat, I said, 'I can't eat these eggs, because you make me puke.' I said, 'If you want the eggs, eat the fuckin' things.' So I moved around, they're all going through their numbers, and one cat runs out of the bedroom yelling, 'I got it, I found it, I got it!' I said, 'What'd you get, man?' He shows the Keystone sergeant, secret-like. Know what he's got? My bottle of sleeping pills. Right? I said to the man, I said, 'If you'd look at the label, it shows my name, the date, and the prescribed dosage.' Oh, no, Keystone won't buy that. He then proceeds to take a capsule out, he breaks it open, he pours some of the powder into his hand, and he does one of *these* numbers!"

He goes through a pantomime of the guy sniffing the powder in his hand, dipping his finger into it, cautiously touching the tip of his finger to the tip of his tongue, then smacking his lips. He underplays the thing and we can't help laughing.

Bobby nods. "You *believe* these guys? So, when he did that —I mean, man, I can't top that. *West Side Story,* right? So, all I could think of, I just said, 'You cats must see a lot of American movies, huh?' They didn't think that was funny. The next cat, he comes out—'What're *these?*' He holds up the bottle like that. So I look. They don't let you touch anything. I said, 'Those are tablets for constipation. They're for your ass. They make you *shit.* No prescription necessary, you can go down to your local apothecary and buy them.' So, next, they're going through our clothes. Like they're looking for twenty million dollars worth of heroin. One cat's an expert on shoes, he tries to slide the heels off, looking for the secret compartment.

"Okay, finally, Keystone asks me who's in the next room. I told him my son. He said, 'Your *son?*' He thought I had some bitch in there. So he goes, 'Open the door.' I said, 'Don't touch that door, man, I'll open the door.' Okay, I open Ron's door. He was still sleeping. I don't know how he managed to sleep through all this, but he did. I woke him up. 'What's the matter, Dad?' 'Nothing, the police are here.' 'What's wrong?' 'Nothing.' So, now, Keystone comes in, starts the whole routine again. Goes straight to Ron's shaving stuff. Sticks his fingers in everything, he even squeezed out the toothpaste. They tore the bed apart, the sheets—it was an unreal experi-

ence. It was almost like a movie. They were into the fuckin'
tea bag Ron used to make tea before going to bed. They took
a knife and opened the tea bag—a wet, used tea bag. They took
a carton of cigarettes, Kents, tore the packs open, even cut
into the filters." He pauses, stubs out his cigarette slowly.

"The bathroom thing," Max reminds him.

"Oh, yeah, the bathroom thing," he says, shaking his head.
"In the middle of all this, before they'd gone into Ron's room,
I asked if it was all right to go in the bathroom and brush my
teeth. Keystone looks around to see if he gets an okay from
everybody. I go to the bathroom door. The door is here." He
demonstrates the layout with a glass of water and the salt and
pepper shakers. "The john itself is behind the bathroom door
and the sink is here. So I'm brushing my teeth, I look in the
mirror, and here's this one cat standing right behind me, right
on my ass, watching every move. Okay, I brushed my teeth.
I didn't piss or anything, I didn't go near the john."

"He wasn't alone in there at all," Cal adds.

"Right. So then they took Ned downtown, and when they
came back again, they had a different search warrant. They'd
changed the warrant from heroin, which they couldn't find, of
course, to *marijuana*. Now, dig this. They went in the bathroom and just happened to find a little bag of cannabis inside
the john. Y'know, inside where the flushing device is? Just
happened to be there. They claimed that I'd stashed it there
when I went to brush my teeth. They claimed I'd taken the
stuff from my bathrobe pocket and stashed it there. Can you
believe that mentality? Plus the fact, there was no way for me
to get behind the door to the john, because there was a cop
on my ass all the time. Well, logic didn't make any fuckin'
difference. We were arrested, taken downtown, and booked.
We got a lawyer, we put up bail, and we left. We flew to
Melbourne and did the concert that night, and it was the best
concert we had the whole time we were in Australia. Despite
all the bad publicity. It was in all the newspapers."

I wait a while, then: "Well, what happened?"

"Nothing. But the damage had already been done."

"Very bad publicity," Cal says, leaning forward. "What actually happened, by the time it came up for trial, he couldn't be there, but he had a lawyer there. He was found guilty *in absentia* and fined fifty bucks. But from my review of the case, very frankly, I don't think it would've even gotten to an indictment stage here. Because it was a public accommodation, y'know, crowds of people going in and out, it could've been stashed there by any previous guest. In my opinion, I think they tried to flake him. Or maybe he *did* stash it there—who the hell knows?"

Bobby smiles at that. "Fabulous attorney I got, right?" Now he gets serious again. "The bad press in this country was one thing, but over *there,* the fuckin' papers—'Bobby Kane arrested on narcotics'—the same size headlines they had in London. But you have to know the press in Australia, man. There was no reason for those stories in the first place, there was absolutely no guilt. I could show you the written statement my lawyer presented, with the truth, which they didn't want to hear. I stated, 'I'm hardly a dope smuggler or user. I'm a man going on fifty-seven years of age. I smoke approximately one pack of cigarettes a day. I don't even drink, except for an occasional glass of wine. I've been married to the same lady for twenty-one years. I have a twenty-year-old son. I'm not some flunky.' "

"Forget it," Cal tells him. "What the hell, that was sixteen years ago."

But he won't forget it, he can't seem to leave it alone. "The mentality of the Australian police and press has to be experienced to be believed. Their big thing in life is getting blind drunk on beer and then beating the shit out of each other. It wasn't always that way over there, but it is now. Their attitude when they ask you questions. Their arrogance when they talk to you. They get personal, very personal. They insult your playing, they make you feel like an asshole. I figured, from the last time I was over there, which was in nineteen fifty-four, that they were terrific people. They couldn't do enough for you back then. Everything was marvelous. This time, forget it. The first interview—I got off the plane after twenty-eight hours, on the flight from London, Ron's falling down, man, he can hardly stand up, he's so tired. Here are all these cats out there with their cameras, and we go into the press room, the first thing the cat says to me, he says, 'Don't you think you're kind of old to be playing drums?' That was the first question. I thought he was kidding at first. I didn't think they were actually taping. 'Is it worth your while? Do you make enough money?' I told one cat on the air, he said, 'Do you make enough money to bring your band over here?' I said, 'No, I just came over here to dig the kangaroos.' "

"It's a simple lack of respect," Max says. "I mean, Bobby's been touring Australia since he was seven years old, he's no newcomer, they owe him more than that. He was a star over there when he was seven, the second-highest-paid child performer in the world."

Bobby shakes his head. "It's not that, Max, they don't know that, they don't give a shit about that. It's a lack of respect for jazz musicians. Period. Doesn't make any difference what your name is. If you're a jazz musician, you're a weirdo, a juicer, a doper. That's the image they have of you. Is he a jazz musician?—get a search warrant, tear up his hotel room, he must have something stashed."

"And it's not limited to Australia," Max says.

"Of course not." Bobby lights another cigarette, glances at Brendan and me. "I don't know how into music you guys are, but have you ever gone to a classical concert and heard people talking out loud during the performance?"

"No," Brendan says. "Very rarely."

"Why don't they?"

Brendan shrugs. "They'd be thrown out."

"Why?"

"For disturbing the majority."

"All right. For disturbing people who enjoy music, who have respect for the music and the musicians. At our club, we have a rule. Silence during the performances. First time it's ever been attempted in a jazz club, to my knowledge. It works. If somebody insists on talking during a performance, we ask him to leave. In fact, we escort him out. It's only happened a few times since we opened, because I think people know how deeply I feel about it. I want silence when we play. I don't ask for that kind of respect—I demand it. Have you guys been to the club?"

"No," I tell him.

"Drop in tonight. I got something for you."

Just like that. That's all he says. And I decide not to push him, because what he's telling me is in his eyes. Brendan picks up on it too. Obviously, this isn't the time or place to go into what he's got. We have a light lunch, during which nothing of any significance is said, shake hands, he tells us to be at the club around nine. We leave and go back to the precinct.

The man's accomplished what he wanted, he's shown us part of himself, sized us up carefully, tested the chemistry, now he's ready for the next step. Still, he'd come on so strong that, in retrospect, it's difficult to understand. And that intrigues me. He could've chosen to do just the opposite, knowing he was about to meet a couple of cops who were complete strangers to him, who wanted to ask him questions about his son. He could've swallowed the frustration about the taxi driver and come on quietly, cautiously, showing control, even if he didn't feel like it, consciously attempting to make at least an agreeable first impression, as most of us do constantly, wearing the guise of social amenity. But, apparently, he'd chosen to come on exactly as he felt—angry as hell. Why? Was that his real personality, away from the bandstands, away from the television cameras? Complicated people resort to complicated camouflage.

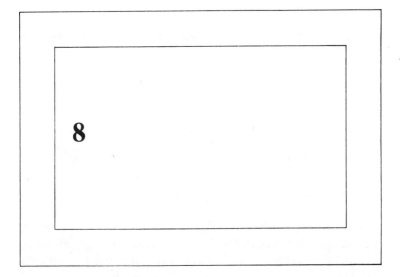

8

$\mathbf{B}$OBBY'S DRUM, a lavishly appointed 400-seat jazz joint, is totally jammed at 9:05, first show scheduled for 9:30, which surprises me, because it's a Wednesday night. These are the real Manhattan night people you hear so much about, mostly young couples, casually but fashionably dressed, money to burn, many having dinner before the show. Always wondered what the hell they do for a living, if anything. There's a line waiting to get into the glass-enclosed cocktail lounge and bar, because the waiters and waitresses are swamped with booze orders from the tables. Even the raised and roped-off VIP area in back is crowded. Nobody's on the bandstand yet, but the heavy stage lights around the ceiling are trained on fifteen "BK" music stands and the white marine pearl sparkles like new, along with the frames of Bobby's drums, which also look new. Brendan and I have a reservation in my name, we ask the maître d' if Bobby or Max have arrived. He nods, escorts us to a table in the VIP section where Max is talking with the headwaiter.

"Glad you could make it." Max stands up, shakes our hands warmly. "Bobby's not here yet, sit down, you had dinner?"

"Yes," Brendan says.

"You want a drink?"

"Maybe later," I tell him.

"Brendan?"

"No, thanks, I'll wait a while."

"Be with you in a minute."

As he continues his conversation with the headwaiter, Brendan and I glance around, take a good look at the place. Big room, indirect lighting, walls are covered with individually lighted aluminum-framed blowups of Bobby in a variety of scenes from his career. Only obvious disadvantage, mirrored pillars block visibility from many seats. Max finishes with the headwaiter, smiles as he sees us taking it all in.

"We opened last April tenth," he says proudly. "It seats four hundred and ten comfortably, but we've had close to four hundred twenty-five some Saturday nights. Food comes from the restaurant upstairs, same food, same drinks."

"You really pack 'em in," Brendan says.

"Yeah, Julie tells me we're sold out for the first show already. Julie, that's the maître d'. That's the way it's been since about June, the first show on week nights is booked solid, then it tapers off some. But on weekends, forget it. Friday, Saturday nights, forget it. Like, on Saturday, we have three shows on Saturday. First show starts at eight forty-five. Before the break, there's a line of couples all the way up the stairs and out into the street. Same thing for the third show, goes on at twelve forty-five. Mostly young people, they get out of the Garden, movies, restaurants around here, anywhere from nine to midnight. Some of them wait on line here close to an hour to get in."

"You must be making money," I tell him.

He nods, smiles, picks up a tent card from the table. It

reads: MUSIC CHARGE $10 PER SHOW. Now he glances around, keeps his voice low. "Well, we give people their money's worth, that's the thing, that's why they keep coming back. All right, each person pays a ten dollar music charge. So, you figure, an average couple comes in here, say tonight, a Wednesday night, not counting the ones that have dinner or a snack, a hamburger. Not counting them. Now, you figure, an average couple will buy maybe a couple of drinks, right? So, we figure, with the music charge, twenty dollars for two, each couple will spend a total of about thirty-two dollars, minimum, not counting tips. Call it sixteen dollars each, minimum. Now, take the first show tonight, we're booked. Say, for round numbers, four hundred people. Multiply that by sixteen dollars. And that's just one show."

"You open six days a week?" Brendan asks.

"Right, we're closed Sundays."

"Nice piece of change," I say.

"Yeah, well, we got a lot of overhead, don't forget. At the end of the week, when I'm figuring it up, salaries and all, it's not that much."

"Do you manage the club?" I ask.

"Yeah, I manage, and I'm Bobby's personal manager. I'm here till two, three o'clock in the morning, I close up the place. Then I work on Bobby's other projects during the day."

One thing about Max, he looks you in the eye and you get an intuitive feeling that there's no bullshit about him. His whole attitude seems to say: "All right, this is me, Max Alexander. If you like me, fine; if you don't, I'm sorry, but that's the way I am. I don't talk the best English, I didn't have a good education, I'm not young or handsome or rich or famous. But I try to be honest most of the time and I know my business and I work very hard at it." First impression, I like the guy.

"Here's Bobby now," he says, standing. "Be right back."

Groups of young people start leaving their tables and heading for the door. I can see Bobby there, talking with the maître d', standing next to the high table that holds the reservations book. Now he's surrounded, he starts signing autographs. Couple of the kids have cameras with strobes and the flashes seem to light up the entire room.

Finally, Bobby makes his way to our table. Max is with him and there's another man by his side who looks to be in his mid-thirties, lean, well-dressed, with thick black hair and a mustache. This guy, the thing that catches my attention first are his eyes: Dark, alert to anyone moving too close to Bobby. Uses his body to maneuver Bobby through the crowd, never actually pushing with his hands, but never stopping his forward motion.

We stand and shake Bobby's hand.

"Rawlings, Thomas, like you to meet Ned Blanchard, my secretary."

Ned gives us a firm grip and smiles. "Glad to meet you."

We all sit down, Bobby and Ned on the opposite side of the table, facing the door. Young couples stand around the table, several autograph books are extended. Ned stands, speaks quietly, moves the people back with his body, never pushing. When he comes back, Bobby asks for a cigarette; it's there in an instant with a gold lighter. Click, flame, click.

Bobby inhales deeply, glances around. "What time is it?"

"Nine-fifteen," Ned tells him.

"SRO for the first set," Max says.

Bobby nods, leans back, looks around, points to somebody at a nearby table, exchanges greetings. Seems completely different from this afternoon, like he'd popped a couple of Valiums. When he smiles in this soft light, he looks much younger, and his clothes enhance the impression—open-necked yellow shirt with matching cardigan trimmed in blue, Cardin logo on the upper left side.

"You guys want a drink?" he asks.

"Later," I tell him.

"How long you been here?"

"Ten minutes."

"What do you think?"

"Nice atmosphere," Brendan says. "Relaxing."

"We're very proud of the place," he says. "Very proud of the way it turned out. It's the first club I've ever had, y'know, first time I've had a home base. I've been on the road all my life. Never had a chance to—y'know, breathe a little."

"Must be quite a satisfaction," Brendan says.

"It is," he says, glancing around again. "I really love the place, y'know, I can't tell you. I mean, okay, we have a lot of noise right now. That's cool, that's fine, they can talk as much as they want before we start playing. Then you get a whole new mood in here, because these people are really into the music. We dim the lights and you can—" He's looking at the front door now and whatever or whoever he sees instantly changes his facial expression. He takes a deep breath with his teeth clenched, stubs out his cigarette, stands up.

Ned's up in a flash, also looking at the front door.

"Come to the dressing room," Bobby tells us. "We can talk."

Ned leads the way as we leave the VIP area. I look toward the front door. Quite a few couples are lined up, waiting to be seated. Julie, the maître d', is talking with a short, stocky man, who's pointing to something in the reservations book. In the light from the high table, I can see the man has a bald pate, long and bushy sideburns that sweep wide over his cheeks, and an old-fashioned handlebar mustache with long, curved ends that make him look faintly ridiculous. But he seems to be speaking with some authority.

I turn to Max as we walk. "What happened?"

"Nothing, that's Bobby's partner."

"The guy talking to Julie?"

"Yeah, he owns half the club, he owns the restaurant."

"They don't get along, huh?"

"No. They don't get along."

Bobby's dressing room is located to the far right of the bandstand, just off a hallway. It's big and seems even bigger because of an enormous floor-to-ceiling mirror that occupies the far wall. Most of the space is devoted to a rectangular "living room" and the actual dressing room is separated by a louvered door. Tan is the dominant color, from dark pine-paneled walls and teakwood cabinets to fitted carpeting, and most of the modern furniture is arranged around a thick glass coffee table with heavy chrome legs. Glass corner tables hold big vases of fresh flowers, the mirrored bar is well stocked, and stereo music plays softly. We all sit around the coffee table.

"First of all," Bobby says, "I have no secrets from Max or Ned, they're like part of the family. You guys have any problem with that?"

"No problem," I tell him.

He sits forward, clears his throat, takes a deep breath. "Here it is up front, all of it: Ron called me this afternoon. Around two forty-five, that's why I was late for lunch. He told me what happened in the barbershop. Now, the story I read in the *Post* late this afternoon was entirely different from what he said, but frankly—you guys read that?"

"Yeah," I say.

"That story was different from what he said, but frankly I believe Ron, I believe he's holding one of your people hostage. Doesn't make any fuckin' difference to him anyway, he's already facing a murder rap. In any event, I think he's had it now. I think he wants to make a deal and give himself up."

I take out my notebook. "Where is he now?"

"I don't know. That's straight. He was calling from a pay phone. We must've talked—I don't know, ten, fifteen minutes, he kept pumping coins in, he wouldn't let me call him back."

"Because he doesn't trust you?" I ask.

"The kid's *scared,* Rawlings! He's scared and confused and we were never real close to begin with! I haven't even *heard* from him in two, three months. He's in real deep, he doesn't know who the fuck to *turn* to now. When he called, he asked to speak with his *mother,* he didn't even want to *talk* to me! He's always been closer to her, all his life. If he'd gotten through to her, he would've asked her for money and a car and God knows what else—and she would've given it to him, all of it. Ned, give me a cigarette, huh?"

Click, flame, click.

He inhales, stares at the carpet, exhales slowly. "Anyhow, she was out shopping, so he was stuck with me. Look, you guys might just as well know this, you'll find it out sooner or later anyway. The truth is, Ron's adopted. Joanne and I adopted him in California when he was three and a half years old. It was a completely legal adoption, we have all the papers, everything, you're welcome to see them. Naturally, we weren't told who his real parents were. The point I'm getting at, he knows I'm not his natural father, he's known since he was seventeen. He had to get a copy of his birth certificate to get in the Army. That's how he found out. State of California had no record of a birth under the name Ronald Drake Laslo— which, as you know, Laslo's my legal name. So we had to tell him the whole thing, show him the papers, everything. It positively blew him away. Seventeen years old and going in the Army, leaving home for the first time, and he gets hit with this. We should've told him years before, but we didn't, we were too fuckin' stupid. So, to answer your question: Trust me? No. No, he doesn't trust me. Not really. Says he does, but he doesn't. Trusts his mother, always has, but not me. To make a long story short, when he called, I didn't jump all over him, I figured that was the last thing he needed, but I gave him my advice. I listened, I listened long and hard, then I advised him to give himself up. And I think he's going to do it."

"How'd you leave it?" Brendan asks.

"He said he wanted to talk to his mother before he did anything. I told him to call back in a couple of hours, she'd be back by then. When I got home from lunch, around four-thirty, Joanne was there, but he hadn't called yet. We had a long talk about it. And she agreed with me. She agreed he should give himself up. So that's it, that's all I know. Joanne's home now waiting. She'll call me here as soon as she talks to him."

I close my notebook. "Would you have any objection to us going over there and briefing your wife about how to handle it? Could make it a lot easier for her."

He thinks about it. "No, I have no objection. Joanne's a night person, she usually stays up till I get home. Ron knows that, of course, so he could call anytime between now and then. By all means, go ahead, I'll call her right now, tell her you're on your way. You know the address?"

"Sure do."

It's raining softly as we drive up to West Sixty-sixth. Eighth Avenue is like black glass, streaked with moving yellows and reds, and the long lines of cars and trucks speed like hell for three or four blocks at a clip with the traffic lights all green in the misty distance. Most of them don't slow at the caution lights, of course, particularly cabs, but simply accelerate to make one more, then slam on their brakes as the lights flash red and skid on the slick street. The rain is so soft that you can't see it clearly until you look at the streetlights, and then, flash, thousands of tiny drops pouring into the long rectangular shafts, floating quietly out of nowhere, slanting down to vanish in the blur of traffic. When we get up to Columbus Circle and continue up Central Park West, Brendan gives me a brief rundown on Joanne Kane. As a jazz buff he knows his share of trivia. Seems her mother was a promising starlet in Hollywood when Joanne was born; gave up her career for the kid. Then Joanne was a promising starlet when she married Bobby in the late 1940s; gave up her career to travel with him.

When we arrive at 9:45, we're expected, doorman tells us to

go straight up, top floor, apartment 34-B. Lobby looks like an ad for an elegant modern hotel. Up we go, smile for the state-of-the-art TV minicam, upper left front corner, wonder if we're in color. Step off, turn left, sink into the carpet down the long hotel-like hall, ring the bell. Chimes. Click-click, double Medeco deadbolts. Joanne keeps the chainlock on as we show gold, introduce ourselves quietly. Come right in, please. Apartment is straight out of *House Beautiful*, obviously decorated by a pro. Three bedrooms (one of which is Bobby's den), three bathrooms, walk-through kitchen with bar, dining room, spacious living room with terrace. They're on the west side of the building and there's a spectacular view of lighted Lincoln Center to the southwest.

After the small-talk prelims, Joanne sits back in the big white couch, almost dwarfed by it, sips a cup of tea: Slim, fragile, strikingly attractive blonde with the face of a girl in her thirties and the hands of a much older woman, wearing a chic denim outfit. Her voice is young, often musical, sometimes hard, and there's a breathless quality when she speaks.

I get down to business as soon as possible: "Mrs. Kane, did your husband explain about the hostage?"

"Yes, he did." She nods, frowns, glances away. "A young —policewoman, isn't it?"

"That's correct. I'm sure you understand that it's absolutely imperative we get her back unharmed. That's our primary objective. Not to get your son, at least not now. But we want the woman back, unharmed, as quickly as that can be arranged. We don't care what it takes."

"I understand."

"Do you believe he'll listen to you?"

She places her cup of tea on the coffee table, stares at it. "I don't know, Detective Rawlings. He's tended to take my advice in the past, at least on important things. But now—I just don't know. Bobby said he sounded very—frightened and confused."

"When he calls," Brendan says quietly, "what we'd like to do, Mrs. Kane, with your permission, we'd like to listen in on your conversation. In other words, we'd like to pick up an extension phone at the exact second you pick up yours. And then just listen. Would that be all right with you?"

"Surely. Would you like to tape record the conversation?"

"Very much," I tell her, "but we didn't have time to get the equipment. We had no idea he'd be calling you tonight."

She nods, stands up quickly. "Bobby has a tape recorder and one of those telephone recording devices—you know, with the suction cup? He uses it for business calls. It's attached to the phone in his den; wait a minute, I'll get it."

As she leaves the room, Brendan and I exchange a look: Classy lady, very cooperative. We can't use the tape in court, of course, these devices are strictly illegal in New York unless the person at the other end knows you're recording, but it's a valuable tool. Chief will be delighted; he routinely records almost all important calls, files 'em away. Wouldn't surprise me if there were more illegal tapes in his files than legal ones.

She comes back quickly with a small tape recorder, the telephone recording device, and a new tape cassette wrapped in cellophane. Places the equipment on the coffee table, clicks out the old cassette, unwraps the new one, clicks it in. All fast and practiced movements, but her hands are shaking noticeably.

Also, there's a slight shake in her voice now: "There's a wall phone in the kitchen with a very long cord. You could plug it on that receiver, then bring it out of the kitchen so we could see each other, and pick up simultaneously with me in here. The living-room telephone is on the end-table over there."

"Excellent, thanks, Mrs. Kane." Brendan grabs the equipment, hustles into the kitchen.

"We really appreciate it," I tell her.

"Well, listen, I can't promise anything. Believe me, I want Ron to release the girl as much as you do, but I'm—I'm afraid

I don't know him very well anymore. We haven't even talked on the phone in a long time now. Months. I still find it extremely difficult to believe he did—all these—things. These terrible things, because he was never inclined that way. Even remotely inclined that way. Honest to God, I don't know what happened to him. I swear to God, I don't. When his marriage started going bad is when it began, I think. He just changed drastically, he became like a stranger to us."

"Mrs. Kane, have you rehearsed in your own mind what you're going to say to him?"

She nods, turns, listens to Brendan testing the device in the kitchen. "Yes. Yes, I have. Bobby says he *thinks* Ron wants to give himself up. Thinks. But Bobby's never had an intuitive sense about Ron like I've had. He's never—somehow he's never been able to read between the lines, y'know? In the past, frequently, it's not what Ron says, it's what he doesn't say that's important. I've tried to listen to what he won't say, then find some way to get at that, to get him to discuss it. So, when he calls—if he calls—the first thing I'm going to do is listen. See what he really has in mind."

"It would help," I tell her, "if you could ask about the detective—her name is Jessica Taylor. If you could simply ask if she's okay. If you could emphasize—"

"Detective Rawlings, sorry for interrupting, but something just occurred to me. Forgive me, I rarely interrupt people, but this could be important. I don't know anything about police work or hostage negotiation or anything, but I have a suggestion that I think might get results. Instead of approaching the whole problem covertly, why don't I just tell it to him straight, the truth?"

"The truth?"

"Yes. That Bobby and I have been approached by the police today, that your number-one priority is to get the girl back, unharmed, as soon as possible, and that you're willing to do anything within reason to make that happen. If I did that, if

I played it honest right from the start, a direct approach, rather than cat-and-mouse, I honestly think he'd be more receptive. I think he'd release the girl much faster. I just have a gut feeling that's what he *needs* right now, for somebody to level with him, to *tell* him what to do, or at least give him a couple of solid alternatives, rather than make some half-ass suggestions that he could interpret as—that could make him even more confused than he is now. What do you think? I mean, he's always trusted me in the past. Plus the fact that he's no fool, he can pick up on when I'm acting and when I'm not."

I think about it, almost automatically reach for a cigar, hesitate. "Mind if I smoke?"

"Not at all, I smoke myself, so does Bobby. As a matter of fact, I'll join you."

I light her cigarette, then my cigar. "Well, you certainly know him better than any of us. If you honestly believe that approach will get results, I have no problem with it."

Brendan comes back. "All set."

"Mrs. Kane's come up with a suggested approach."

"Yeah, I heard part of it."

"What do you think?" she asks.

Brendan sits down, takes out a cigar. "I have just one question, Mrs. Kane. In your opinion, is there any possibility you might scare him off that way?"

"Well, let's face it, obviously I can't be one hundred percent sure. But knowing Ron's personality as well as I do—or I should say, as well as I used to—I think we stand a better probability of getting through to him. As I said earlier, we could give him several positive alternatives. What specific alternatives would you suggest?"

"First of all," I tell her, "I don't think he's going to give himself up just like that. I've never bought that. I think we can rule it out. I believe he'll be looking to deal. Deal from strength, because he's holding the cards at this point. So you can tell him this: Number one, if he wants cash in return for

Jessica, unharmed, that can be arranged. Number two, if he wants cash plus safe passage out of the country in return for Jessica, unharmed, that can probably be negotiated. If he's got another idea, if he wants to plea-bargain, reduce the murder-one charge to, say, as low as involuntary manslaughter, all that is possible, providing we get Jessica back unharmed. Brendan?"

"Well, okay, I think you covered the basic deals he'd be looking to make. One point that should certainly be stressed is Jessica's condition. Before we agreed to any kind of deal, we'd have to speak with her on the phone. Long enough to determine that she's all right. If he's hurt her, if he's seriously injured the girl, we've got a whole different situation. He won't be on the phone with you long enough for us to run a trace, he's too smart for that, so you'll have to make your points fairly quickly."

Goes on like that. Exactly 10:16, the telephone rings. Brendan runs to the kitchen, turns on the recorder, appears behind the kitchen bar with his finger on the receiver's disconnect button. Mrs. Kane sits by the end-table, hand on the receiver, ready.

"On the count of three," Brendan says. "One, two, three."

Here's the verbatim transcription:

"Hello."

"Did he call yet?"

"Oh, Bobby. No, not yet."

"Shit."

"We're still waiting."

"Just finished the first set."

"I'll call you just as soon as he calls."

"Okay, I'll get off. Be real firm with him, huh?"

"I promise. Just like we discussed."

"Good. Take care."

"Bye-bye."

We play it back to make certain the suction cup is placed

high enough on the back of the receiver to pick up clearly. It is. Both voices come across loud and clear. Then, at 10:22, the real thing:

"Hello."

"I heard two clicks. Who's there?"

"Two detectives, Ron, but they're—"

"Identify yourselves, assholes!"

"Thomas, Nineteenth."

"Mom, get off the line, huh?"

"Are you all right?"

"I'm—okay."

"How's the girl?"

"Fine. Please get off the line. I gotta talk to this guy fast, they're tracing this."

"I love you, Ron." Click.

"All right, Thomas, listen *hard,* I'm only gonna say it once: Five hundred thousand cash, all one hundred dollar bills. That's five thousand bills. Each set of fifty will have an entirely different serial sequence. That's a total of one thousand different serial sequences. Understand?"

"Yeah. That'll take time."

"I know that, asshole. Because you're gonna record the serial numbers. Friday morning, ten o'clock. One large suitcase. Leave it with the doorman in the lobby."

"This building?"

"Right. Doesn't make any fuckin' difference where I pick it up. You have me followed, I'll wander around for *days!* Meantime, Jessica Taylor's locked in a trunk. She'll suffocate while you're tailing me. You understand that?"

"No deal. We don't know she's alive."

"I haven't *finished,* you fuckin' moron! Have a listen."

"It's Jessica, I'm okay. Just do exactly—"

"Jessica, what *time* is it?"

"—what he tells you, he's desperate, he—"

"What *time* is it?"

"—means what he says."

"You hear that, Thomas?"

"No deal. It's a tape recording."

"Of *course* it's a tape recording, you fuckin' moron! I can't bring her out on the *street* to a fuckin' *pay phone!* She's alive. She's locked in a trunk, she's safe."

"No deal until we speak to her live."

"All right. Tomorrow morning, Vadney's office, eleven o'-clock. He gets one question. She gets five seconds to answer. Deal?"

"No deal. Tomorrow morning at eleven, plus Friday morning at nine. Vadney's office. She gets fifteen seconds each time."

"No way. Five seconds each time."

"Ten seconds each time. Deal?"

"Deal."

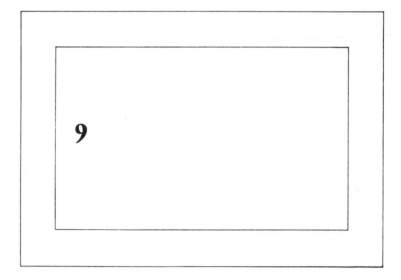

9

CHIEF'S POSITIVELY ECSTATIC when he hears the tape, 9:15 next morning. Listens to it a total of seven times with Brendan and me, then twice more with his Sony Walkman stereo headset, big mitts pressed over the earphones, brows knitted, tongue out slightly, to see if he can pick up any background noises that might possibly prove valuable. Man's in such good spirits he throws caution to the wind, breaks one of his primary rules of office decorum, actually allows Brendan and me to have a cup of coffee right at the conference table. No cigars, of course, he wouldn't have his space violated with a known carcinogenic, not to mention stinking up the office, but we feel we've made a genuine breakthrough anyway. Laslo's scheduled to call at eleven, so a whole series of emergency measures are initiated. First off, Chief gets on the horn with some bigwig at the New York Telephone Company, tries to determine if there's any brand-new space-age advanced electronic computer wizardry, experimental or classified or whatever, that would make it possible to trace a call made from a pay phone somewhere in the city in roughly fifteen seconds. Bigwig doesn't even answer him. Breaks up laughing. Can't help himself. Roars. Brendan and I pretend we can't hear. Chief hangs up, *bang,* then yells a string of cathartic expletives at the trembling receiver.

Operating on the proven principle that the fewer people who know what's going on in any given emergency situation, the less likely it is to get totally fucked up, Chief decides to limit the latest hostage intelligence to Brendan and me, Marty Shugrue, Dave Pearson, Emergency Service Division Commander Jim Mairs, and—reluctantly but necessarily now that a ransom demand has been made—Special Agent Harvey Katz of the FBI.

Where, you ask, does NYPD get its hands on $500,000 in $100 bills with special serial-number specifications? Simple. Since a kidnapping is involved, a hostage is being held, a ransom demand made, and since at 10:15 this morning the FBI's mandatory twenty-four hour waiting period will have expired (in the old days it was seventy-two hours), Chief will merely pick up the phone, speak with genial Harvey Katz over at 26 Federal Plaza, update him on the basics, and request the $500,000, thereby setting in motion a virtual epidemic of Tylenol headaches. Katz, in turn, will call the Treasury Department, speak to Henry Orloski, Controller of the Currency, make the official request—reason classified—which is all it takes to set dozens of federal accountants and vault people in frantic motion. Mr. Orloski will also make the arrangements for a Brink's armored truck to transport the cash to One Police Plaza.

But it's only 9:40 now and Vadney's pumped up with an idea he's almost certain could lead to Laslo's apprehension within an hour after he picks up the cash tomorrow morning. Won't tell us exactly what it is yet, first he wants to pick the brains of ESD Commander Jim Mairs ("pronounced Mars," he reminds us, "like the planet he flew in from!"), whose office is just down the hall, and who happens to be the resident genius in state-of-the-art undercover electronic gadgetry. Calls him, asks if the three of us could drop in a minute to jaw. Mairs says sure, all he's got are a dozen routine emergencies this morning.

Down the hospital-like hall we go, Chief's steel-tipped heels clicking hurriedly on the gleaming floor. Mairs's assistant greets us in her office, unusually attractive young blonde kid, glasses, obviously high IQ. Chief calls her "Moneypenny." Gets his rocks off when he calls her that, knows it drives her up the wall.

"Hey, Moneypenny," he says. "How's yer Hot-Cross buns today?"

Her eyelids go half-mast. "How deep is the snow on a vampire's grave?"

"Aw, shoot, Moneypenny, when y'gonna gimme a break?"

"Chief Vadney," she says quietly. "Imagine, if you can, a sparrow standing at the apex of an enormous solid-granite mountain."

"Yeah, okay. What about it?"

"Now imagine, if you can, that sparrow starting to rub the underside of its beak against the apex of that solid-granite mountain."

"Yeah. So what?"

"When that sparrow has worn down that solid-granite mountain to ground level, Chief Vadney, that's when I'll give you a break."

He smiles. "Y'hear the one about the seagull and the nude sunbather?"

She rolls her eyes.

"You'll love this one, Moneypenny. See, there's this gorgeous nude sunbather on this beach, and a seagull sashays up to her, and he says, 'Hey, honey, how's yer ass?' She looks at him, she says, 'Shut up!' He says, 'Yup, mine is too, must be the salt air!' " Chief breaks up, he's leaning over her desk, he's laughing so hard his eyes are watering.

She gives him a slow Mona Lisa smile. "That's really terrific, Chief. You're getting away from your scatological fixation." Dismisses him with a nod toward Mairs's closed door. "He's expecting you."

Must say, walking into Mairs's office is always a bit unsettling to me. Chief calls him "Commander Cuckoo" behind his back, an impression I don't happen to share, but if you walked in here as a complete stranger and glanced around, you might choose your words with care. Floor-to-ceiling bookshelves overflowing with hardcovers and paperbacks, a collection of scale-model classic cars and locomotives and unopened Olympia beer cans, all-American-guy stuff, but cleverly combined with a veritable menagerie of decidedly cuckoo items. Like a preserved bat hanging upside-down from the gnarled limb of a half-dead geranium plant. Like a preserved frog that was flattened by a truck. Like a tiny wire cage hanging from a preserved venus flytrap near the window. The tiny wire cage has a black cloth draped over it with a white inscription: R.I.P. Know what was in that tiny wire cage? Or, rather, what's still in that tiny wire cage, for all I know? A pet cockroach named Quint II. Swear to God. Healthy little creature too, last I saw it, well-fed, bright-eyed, slime-backed, hairy-legged. Passed away just last year of some strange unknown malady. Stricken in its grime, so to speak, same as its mother, Quint I, who'd laid eggs in the cage before her untimely demise. Never had the joy of seeing her sole surviving progeny. Story goes, Mairs took the youngster's passing very hard. Went home, got a little drunk, played Bach's *Toccata and Fugue in D Minor* on his organ all night. Neighbors finally had to call the police. That's how we got the story, that's how we know it's true.

Irony is, Jim Mairs is one of the most talented and decorated cops in the department. Dartmouth graduate, finished first in his class at the Police Academy. Looks, acts, speaks like a college professor, that's the dominant impression he gives. Authoritative without the abrasiveness of your standard MBA corporate prick. Hates to be thought of as an intellectual, but he is, in the best sense of the word.

He's on the phone as we walk in, shirtsleeves, conservative tie (four-in-hand knot, never windsor), high forehead that seems even higher now the brown hair is receding, green eyes penetrating as ever, lean oval face starting to show the mileage of mid-forties. Smiles as he motions us to sit, that special smile he reserves for meetings with Vadney, entertainment high point of any day.

Only two visitors' chairs in the office, so I quickly choose the window ledge. As Mairs writes something down, I study the preserved venus flytrap plant from which hangs the object of my insatiable detective curiosity. Now, nonchalantly, I turn my wristwatch to the light, covertly use a forefinger to lift the black R.I.P. cloth, take a quick peek inside. Sorry I did. Quint II is still in residence, what remains of him, on his back, once-hairy legs straight up, frozen in rigor mortis *cucaracha.* Chief catches me in the act, frowns, shakes his head just perceptively in stern rebuke, eyes wide, horrified at such indiscretion in the presence of the bereaved. Less than thirty seconds later, his curiosity finally wins. Eyes dart between me and the cage, nods to ask the silent question: "Is he really *in* there?" I close my eyes in disdain, refuse to confirm or deny such necrophiliac inquisition. Now he glares at me, ordering, demanding, furious at such blatant insubordination. I figure, fuck him, let him suffer. Milking my moment of power, I reach in my pocket slowly, take out my pack of Dutch Masters panatellas, select one, move it across my nose to savor the rich aroma, start to bite off the end, hesitate, glance over at him, hold the stogee to my lips with the silent question: "Mind?" Smirks, nods permission; difficult compromise, but he's got to know the answer before Mairs gets off the phone. I figure, no hurry, prolong the suspense. Slowly, meticulously, I bite off the end, plunk it in the ashtray on the desk, light up as smokefully as possible, face obscured in clouds of mystery. Take a few puffs, blow circles toward the ceiling, watch them billow ominously over in the vicinity of his air space where, in due time, invisible rain might violate those below. Okay, time to pay off. Right hand held from Mairs's view, I point to the cage, then jerk my thumb up. Chief's eyes widen, frown follows as his gaze goes inward, mind groping to visualize the deceased. Nostrils twitch involuntarily.

Finally, Mairs finishes his conversation, hangs up, apologizes for the delay, reaches for his Marlboros. Chief explains the basics of the hostage situation and ransom demand. As usual, Mairs listens attentively, never interrupts, takes a few notes. Brendan, sitting near the chief, can smell my delightful smoke, wants a cigar desperately, but doesn't dare light up. Keeps glancing at me with envious eyes. I puff away happily.

Basics over, Chief takes his Sony TCM-600 from his back pocket (he's replaced the Laslo tape with a new one), places it on the desk, mike toward Mairs, clears his throat, presses the record button. "Jim, remember in the old days we used to track with this old-fashioned gizmo—I think it was called a 'homing device' or something like that?"

"Yes."

"I haven't used one of those things in years now. Refresh my memory, how'd that work?"

"It was a simple battery-powered acoustic mechanism. Permitted navigation toward an objective by maintaining a constant bearing on a radio beam."

"Yeah. Right. I'm—I'm afraid I haven't kept up to speed on all this space-age computer revolution stuff going on today. Changes too fast for me. What's the high-tech counterpart of that device called now?"

"A homing device."

Chief hesitates, smiles. "You puttin' me on, buddy?"

"No. That's what it's still called by most of us. It's just a bit more sophisticated today, that's all. For example, the homing device itself is powered by a lithium battery. But it still operates on the same basic principle."

"Use it much?"

"Occasionally."

"Okay, here's our problem, Jim. Now, as far as the ransom pick-up, we're up against a fourteen-year veteran cop here. Ex-cop, I should say. I mean, he knows all the tricks. Knows 'em cold. We try to follow him in any conventional surveillance pattern, he'll be on to us in nothin' flat. I can't risk it. Jessica, she'll be locked in a trunk. He says if he even so much as smells a tail, he'll wander around for days, Jessica will eventually smother to death. So he's got us by the short and curlies there. And he knows it. Question: If we managed to conceal a homing device in the suitcase that'll hold the cash —he specified one suitcase—if we did that, is there any way he could detect the thing? I mean, other than ripping the case apart and finding it?"

"He'd have to know the radio frequency we'd use and he'd have to get access to relatively sophisticated equipment. For example, on the frequency, we could go to VHF, UHF, SHF, or even EHF."

Chief frowns. "Y'lost me on those last two."

"SHF, superhigh frequency, that's three to thirty gigahertz. EHF, extremely high frequency, is thirty to three hundred gigahertz, the highest known frequency."

"What the fuck's a gigahertz?"

"A unit of frequency equal to about one billion hertz."

"Uh-huh." Chief looks at his Sony, checks to see that his new Maxell UD-6o tape cassette is rolling. "And just for the record—sorry about this, Jim, but I gotta explain this to others—just for the record, what's a—how would you define a hertz?"

"A unit of frequency of a periodic process equal to one cycle per second. Named after Heinrich R. Hertz, a German physicist who discovered it and developed it in the late nineteenth century. Not related to Hertz Rent-A-Car, as far as I know."

Chief smiles at that. "Leave it to the Krauts. So, in other words, if we used like SHF or EHF, Laslo couldn't possibly have the kinda high-tech equipment to detect the thing?"

"It's very unlikely, but we don't know his circumstances."

"Jim, far as we know, this sucker don't have a bucket to dump in or a window to chuck it outa."

"Assume exactly the opposite," Mairs says softly. "By this time, in this city, he could've stolen a great deal of money. But to get to the point, I agree that a homing device seems like a plausible idea. The only problem I have with it, I suspect Laslo's anticipated us. In my judgment, putting myself in his place, I believe he probably plans to pick up the suitcase, then transfer the cash to another receptacle immediately. We're talking about a fourteen-year veteran ex-cop who's going to anticipate—*try* to anticipate—every trick in the book. However, you might want to consider this: ESD has a recently developed homing device that's about the size of a quarter and just about as *thin*. Naturally, the cash will be tied in many individual bundles. So you might want to consider placing the device *inside* one of the bundles. He'd discover it sooner or later, but not necessarily when he makes that first rough count. When he counts it the first time—and remember, this is strictly conjecture—when he counts it the first time he probably won't remove the bank seals that tie each bundle. He'll flip through each bundle to make sure the bills are authentic and to check that you followed his instructions about breaking up the serial-number sequences. We could glue the homing device to the center of two bills, top and bottom, then place it in the middle of one of the bundles. That would buy us time. *Where* he does the initial count is a critical factor. When we determine that the homing device is no longer moving, that the container is stationary for, say, at least five or ten minutes, do we move in on him *then?* Think about that carefully. Because he may do that first count at a considerable distance from where he's got Jessica. Just to be certain the cash is genuine and the serial-number sequences are exactly as he specified. *Then* he might go to Jessica. I realize this is all hypothetical, but, to repeat, I'm trying to put myself in his place."

"So you'd wait till he makes the *second* stop?" Chief asks.

Mairs takes a drag on his cigarette. "Look at it from his perspective. He might stop somewhere—a great distance from Jessica—just to see what *happens.* If he's in a vehicle of some kind, and I assume he will be, a stolen vehicle, he might drive miles and miles, all over the city, then just pull over and stop. Just to see if we've somehow managed to tail him. He says he'll have Jessica locked in a trunk of some kind?"

"Yeah," Chief says. "That's what really worries me."

"Okay, again, look at it from his angle. It's not necessarily *true* he'll have her in a trunk just because he said he will. In fact, if I were him, I positively would *not* lock her up someplace where she could smother, because the time element would then work *against* me. I'd want all the time I could get to determine that I wasn't being tailed. Also, a car or a van or whatever, parked in a side street or a public garage, would be an ideal place to make a fast first count of the money. Then —then and only then—would I even consider going near Jessica."

"Question, Jim," I say. "Once he's got the money and he's sure we're not tailing him, why would he go to Jessica at *all?* Why not leave town, telephone us, tell us where we can find her?"

"Good question," Chief says.

Mairs stubs his cigarette out slowly. "Excellent question. He might very well do just that. It's logical, it's safe, he could put a lot of distance between us before he called. At least he'd *think* he was putting distance between us. If he played it that way, we'd be home free. We'd get Jessica back and, theoretically, he'd still have the homing device. We'd keep the signal in range no matter where he went, we'd always be following at a very safe distance. He wouldn't be dumb enough to go to an airport, train station, or bus terminal in the tri-state area, he knows our saturation routine too well for that. But he might try it if he was well out of the tri-state area. For example, if he decided to head northeast up through Connecticut, Massachusetts, wherever, with the idea of getting on a plane somewhere, we'd still be with him. In the meantime, he'd have to stop sometime, for gas, food, rest, and we'd take him with the help of the local police. At the earliest time possible, in the least crowded place."

"Jim," Brendan says. "Hate to ask this, but you've got a lot more experience in hostage situations than we do. In your opinion, is there a reasonable probability this guy might actually kill Jessica?"

He glances out the window. "All right. Okay. We might just as well face the idea up front, unpleasant as it is. Personally, I don't believe there's a high probability. Unless something happens, he's cornered, there's no way out, and in that situation I think he might kill her and kill himself. Keep in mind, we're dealing with someone who's mentally ill, who's already killed one woman. But, no, I honestly don't believe there's a high probability of that."

"Frankly," Chief says, "what worries me more than that is what he's doin' to her now, physically. He's holed up with her someplace and he's got a lot of time on his hands. Given his personality, given what we know about him, what he's done to other women, God only knows how many others, this fucker's like a walkin' Spanish Fly. All the weird shit he's pulled on these kids, S-and-M, B-and-D, that's what I can't seem to get out of my mind."

There's a silence. A long silence.

Chief looks at his watch. "He's scheduled to call my office

at eleven sharp, Jim, we gotta get back. He says I'm allowed to ask Jessica one question. She's got exactly ten seconds to answer. That's it until tomorrow morning when he calls at nine. Same routine, I get one question, she gets ten seconds to answer. Any suggestions?"

Mairs sits back, thinks about it. "Obviously, the only important consideration is Jessica's well-being, her physical condition. If I were you, Chief, I'd play it straight, I wouldn't ask anything that sounded even remotely like a trick question. Because, again, anticipating this guy, I assume he'll listen to the question, then relay it to her. Ten seconds later, he'll hang up."

"Uh-huh," Chief says. "I mean, like, what would you ask?"

"Something that couldn't possibly be answered with a 'Yes' or 'No.' Something that'd give you at least some insight into how she's being treated."

"Uh-huh. Like what?"

"Like: 'Jessica, describe your physical condition.' "

Chief stands. "Jim, appreciate your help, goes without sayin'. We need your expertise from here on out, buddy-boy, I'm countin' on you."

"Only too glad to help."

"Stop in just before eleven?"

"I'll be there."

Now's the best time to tell you about Vadney's new executive secretary. I've been saving this. Last couple of years, Chief had a kid named Steve Adair who was one hell of a good typist and all but suffered a nervous breakdown. Anyhow, story goes, Chief hires a Kelly Girl while he conducts interviews for a replacement. Posts the required NYPD job description, gets the usual flood of applicants from the department. This is in August, last August. After three weeks and close to forty interviews, he decides to go outside, places a carefully worded ad in the *New York Times*. What he wants, of course, is somebody to equal or even surpass Moneypenny in looks and brains, but his wife Samantha insists the successful candidate *must* be a married woman, preferably with grown children. That rules out youngsters like Moneypenny. Chief figures, okay, if he can't have her real young, then he wants the classiest, brightest, most eloquent, most efficient gal he can find in the open market. Two weeks and three dozen interviews later, in pops this knockout of a lady named Doris Banks. Early forties, blonde, hazel-eyed, about five-four, French-Canadian stock, married to a successful executive. Both originally from Canton, Ohio, moved to New York about twenty years ago, have a grown daughter. Business experience? Get a load of this. Her last job, she was executive secretary to the president of American Airlines. Yeah! When American moved its corporate headquarters to Dallas around four, five years ago, she decided to retire. Didn't have to work anyhow, her husband was loaded by then. Now, this year, she decides she wants to look around again, she's bored. Ad in the *Times* doesn't mention NYPD, just gives a box number. When Doris finds out the position is executive secretary to the NYPD Chief of Detectives, she laughs out loud. Goes for an interview anyhow, figures it's fabulous fodder for the cocktail-party circuit. Vadney takes one look at this Tiffany-type class, he's drooling his molars, he's squirting his knickers, his eyes look like the Duke's when he finally won the Oscar for *True Grit.* Doris, she's supercool to the whole idea. Chief wines and dines her for two solid weeks, promises her the moon with him barking at it. First week in October, just after this case begins, Doris takes the job. Strictly on a trial basis. Probationary period for Vadney. Me, I happen to like this little lady. If I had to sum her up in one sentence, I'd say this: Doris don't take no shit from *nobody.*

Give you an idea of what I mean. After the meeting with Jim Mairs this morning, we walk back to Vadney's office, which means we pass through Doris's office in the reception area just outside. Used to look like your standard NYPD waiting room. Not now. Picture this: You walk in, the ugly fluorescent overhead lights are off, replaced by the warm golden glow of three black-marble lamps on three white-marble tables in three corners. Other corner, far left, occupied by Doris's new glass-and-chrome desk. All the ratty furniture has been replaced by elegant matching white couches and chairs. Now there's a cozy sitting area to the right with a new glass-and-chrome coffee table. Know what's on that coffee table? Strictly *current* copies of *Time, Newsweek, New York, Geo, New Yorker,* this morning's final editions of the *Times* and *Journal.* Plus clean cut-glass ashtrays. Walls? Oil paintings of a variety of New York street scenes, tastefully framed, individually lighted. Carpet? Same light-gray job, but professionally cleaned, spotless now. Who paid for all this? Doris's husband Will. Yeah! He loves the lady, money's no object to make her happy, what can I tell you? And keep in mind, she's accepted the job on a trial basis. Consensus opinion around headquarters, if Doris splits, Chief's waiting room will be as empty as his head.

So now we walk in, Doris is typing what looks to be at least 120 wpm on her new black IBM Correcting Selectric III. Glances up, smiles, lustrous blonde hair, subtle makeup, conservative but fashionable designer outfit. Hands over a stack of telephone messages.

Chief's so pleased with her whole scene he can't suppress the all-out left-sided molar shower every time he sees her. Keeps his voice very low and dignified. "Doris, uh, as you know, Laslo's due to call at eleven sharp."

"Yes, sir."

He glances at his watch. "Ten thirty-five now. At ten fifty-nine and thirty seconds, please don't pick up any calls. I'll handle this one myself."

"Chief," she says softly. "May I offer an opinion?"

"Oh, yeah, please *do.*"

"That's poor psychology."

"Huh?"

"Gives him the edge."

"Yeah?"

"Make him wait."

"Huh?"

"Make him sweat."

"Yeah?"

"He'll be at a pay phone with Jessica. When he calls, I'll let it ring three times, then pick up and say, 'Chief Vadney's office; hold on, please.' Click. He doesn't get one word in." She glances at her gold Piaget watch. "Exactly thirty seconds later, click: 'Chief Vadney's office; may I help you?' You'll have the clear psychological edge."

"Yeah, huh?"

She smiles. "He'll yell. Predictably. 'This is Ron Laslo! Put me through fast!' I'll pause. 'Mr. Laslo, sir, there's no need to raise your voice in that manner. Chief Vadney's expecting your call. One moment, please.' I buzz you, tell you it's him. You activate your tape recorder and pick up. Calmly, as usual. Grace under pressure."

Chief hesitates, frowns, manages a half-smile. "But, Doris, uh, suppose he just—suppose he just hangs up?"

"He won't. I guarantee it. Operate from a position of strength, Chief. Strength."

Chief frowns, nods, straightens up, adjusts his black-holstered Smith & Wesson .38 Chief's Special on his right rear hip, adjusts his black-holstered Motorola walkie-talkie on his left rear hip. "Doris, appreciate your help, goes without sayin'. Uh, please hold all calls till after Laslo's. Oh, and I'm expectin' Mairs to join us shortly, send him right in."

"Certainly."

He turns to Brendan and me. "You guys want some more coffee?"

"Love it."

"Love it."

Now he turns to Doris, starts to give the coffee order.

"Gentlemen," she interrupts quietly, "the coffee machine is just down the hall to your left." Goes back to her typing.

Tell you what, this Doris Banks is something. Class act all the way. Kid don't take no shit from *nobody*.

Laslo calls almost exactly at eleven. Vadney, Mairs, Brendan, and I stare at the flickering top button on the chief's console. Flickers quickly, silently, three long times. Now the light turns steady as Doris answers, changes to a slow flash as she puts him on hold. All four of us check the second-hands on our watches. Exactly thirty-one seconds later, button light goes steady as she takes him off hold, gets a yelling earful, I assume, gives him a quick lesson in telephone etiquette, I'm sure. Puts him on hold again, hits the intercom buzzer.

"Laslo on line one."

"Thanks." Chief presses the record button on his Sony, which is positioned on the conference table directly in front of the telephone squawk-box speaker, so we can all hear. Now he presses the line-one button and the squawk-box button simultaneously. "Hello."

"Ask your question, asshole! *Fast!*"

"Jessica, describe your physical condition."

Laslo's voice is hard to hear now: "He wants to know your physical condition. You got ten seconds. No tricks. Go."

Jessica sounds hoarse but relatively calm: "I'm weak and stiff, but I'm okay. He's kept me tied up and blindfolded all the time, in the nude, and gagged except when he feeds me. I've been—"

Click.

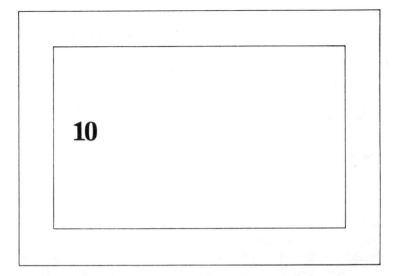

10

BACK AT THE PRECINCT, about 2:30 that afternoon, we get a call from Bobby Kane. Says his father called him about ten minutes ago and told him something that we might want to check out. His father, Harry, who's eighty-seven years old and lives out in Brighton Beach, Brooklyn, says Ron came to his apartment around one o'clock this afternoon and borrowed a large suitcase. Naturally, his dad doesn't know about the hostage situation because the information wasn't released to the press and Bobby didn't want to upset him, at his age, by telling him. Apparently, Ron and his "grandfather" have always been very close. Of course, the old man knows Ron's a fugitive, he'd read all about that in the papers, so he tried to talk him into giving himself up and getting help. They didn't talk long, Ron was in a hurry, he just took the suitcase, thanked him, promised to keep in touch, and left. Bobby thinks it might be worth our while to go out and talk with his dad, see if he can remember anything that could be of help. We tell him absolutely, we'll leave right away, should be there in forty-five minutes to an hour. He gives us the address, apartment number, telephone number, explains that after his dad retired from vaudeville, about forty-five years ago, he went back to his legal name, Laslo. Harry Laslo. Says he'll call and tell him we're coming.

Fastest way to get to Brighton Beach from midtown Manhattan is by subway, so Brendan and I take the Lexington Avenue IRT downtown to Fourteenth Street, change to the BMT line, then take the QJ train all the way out. About forty-five minutes later, we rattle and sway from underground darkness into bright daylight in south Brooklyn and soon the tracks are elevated high over the little communities that make up the "real" New York, a completely different world from Manhattan. Brighton Beach is the station just before Coney Island and the elevated tracks extend directly over the main drag, Brighton Beach Avenue, which is lined with hundreds of small stores—delicatessens, groceries, poultry markets, pizza parlors, candy stores, laundries, fruit stands, clothing stores, fish markets, bars, and record stores blaring rock. Sidewalks are crowded and there are lots of kids around because school's out for the day. Looking south down the narrow, shady, apartment-lined streets, we can see the ocean. I know the area well, because my aunt had been confined to a nursing home nearby and I visited her every week during the summer of 1971 before she died.

Down in the street, I'm again aware of the familiar combination of smells and noise and music, which brings back memories. When the traffic light changes and we cross the street under the elevated tracks, it's shady and cool. Train roars overhead, an express; noise drowns out the music, patterns of sunlight flicker on the asphalt.

Harry Laslo lives just south of the elevated, on one of the streets leading to the sea, lined with attractive old apartment houses. His building, 3110 Brighton Seventh Street, is six stories of gray-brown brick with a latticework of brown fire escapes down the front. Can't help but notice how clean all the windows are, like the residents take special pride in their building. White and gray arched entrance has tall double doors with glass so clean it reflects our images like a mirror. There's no doorman. We go in the vestibule, press the bell to apartment 4-B. Inside door buzzes almost immediately.

Take the elevator up, ring the bell, hear footsteps approach. Two deadbolt locks click and Harry Laslo swings open the door, a short, lean man, completely bald, wearing black horn-rimmed glasses with lenses just thick enough to distort his dark eyes. We introduce ourselves and show our gold. He shakes our hands and smiles warmly.

"Come in, come in," he says. "What the hell took you so long?"

"We took the BMT," I tell him.

"Well, that explains it!" He laughs then, quickly, easily, looking up at me, glasses catching the light.

A small white-haired woman walks down the hall, looks to be in her mid-sixties, so I know she's not Bobby's mother. Her glasses have three-quarter frames and she's stylishly dressed in a white blouse and finely checked Chanel-type suit.

"This is Leslie," Harry says. "The French bombshell."

She smiles, shakes our hands, speaks with traces of a French accent. "Don't pay any attention to him. He's gone crazy in his old age. Regression to adolescence, I think you call it."

The walls of the long hallway are covered with framed photographs and memorabilia, and Harry shows us a selection before we go inside. Some are photos from his own vaudeville career, but the majority cover Bobby's career, from the age of eighteen months to the present, like a one-man show at a gallery, photos from all over the world, and he identifies virtually every person, the cities, countries, theaters, and approximate dates. I suppose he's recited the same information to so many people over the years that it's not really the surprising feat of memory it seems, but it's the way he does it that intrigues me, the gravel in his voice, the way he touches the glass of the frames ever so gently, the way he pauses and looks up at us for our reaction. To the best of my knowledge, nobody in my family ever lived to be eighty-seven, and I don't think I'd ever observed anyone of that age looking at a record of his life in frozen time, which is what photographs essentially are, to me anyway. Without them, how much would we actually recall in such vivid detail? How much would be lost? How much of time past would be rationalized? The written word can sometimes capture part of the quality of our lives, and even add a reflective dimension, which photos can't do, but how many of us keep a written record? How many of us will be able to remember clearly what it was like to be young and what we did and who our friends were and how we really looked and how our children looked and changed over the years, without the aid of photographs, however posed, however amateur? I've always been attracted to photography, but I leave that hallway with a new optimism about it, seeing the range of emotions it can trigger in a person of that age, especially the happiness.

Living room's small and comfortable, overlooking the street, and there are more photos on all the tables, of course. Mrs. Laslo serves coffee and we all exchange small-talk, mostly about Bobby and his new club and how well he's doing. Finally, I get out my notebook and pen, try to ease into some questions about Ron's visit.

"Mr. Laslo, Bobby tells us Ron was here this afternoon."

"Yeah." He stands, goes into the kitchen, comes back with an ashtray, places it on the coffee table between Brendan and me. "Please feel free to smoke, if you want."

"Thank you," I tell him. "Maybe later."

Sits down, sips his coffee, seems quite nervous now. "Tell me about yourself, Detective Rawlings. How long you been in the department now?"

"Twenty-eight years."

"Yeah? And how old're you? If you don't mind my asking."

"No, sir. Just turned fifty."

"Fifty? Hell, you're a young man! Detective Thomas, you about the same?"

"I'm forty-six, sir."

"And how long you been a cop?"

"Nineteen years, sir."

He exchanges a glance with Leslie, clears his throat. "You guys like to walk?"

I shrug. "Sure."

Looks at his watch. "I take my afternoon constitutional every day about this time. Let's go down to the boardwalk, I'll show you guys around, we can talk."

Something's happening here, I'm not sure what. Could be the subject of Ron is too painful for Leslie, or maybe we're just getting into it too fast, but somehow I have a gut feeling it's more complicated than that.

Outside, he seems more relaxed. Uses a cane, but says he only needs it to beat away the girls and autograph hounds. Walks at a good clip and seems to enjoy the sun and the fresh ocean smell of the air. We head south to Brighton Court, where the outside swimming pool of the YM-YWHA is closed till next summer, cross the street and turn left past the clean, tan, three-story YM-YWHA building, then right on Coney Island Avenue and up on the enormous boardwalk that extends for many miles, all the way to the amusement park at Coney Island, which we can see in the distance. To our left, the wide beach is almost empty and the glare from the sea is very strong.

"I wasn't born around here," Harry tells us. "I was born in Schenectady, New York. Yeah, Schenectady, December tenth, eighteen ninety-five. Two months more, if I make it, eighty-eight years old I'll be. Eighty-eight years old."

"Where did you get into show business?" Brendan asks.

"I worked with a fella by the name of Kelly in Albany.

We're playing—you know, clubs, little things, around. Five dollars a night apiece, things like that. And then, it was 'Kane and Kelly' then."

"How old were you?" I ask.

"I was about—I was a hoofer, strict dancing act, you know? I was about sixteen. And we went on there for a couple of years. About the time I was eighteen, I came down to New York, by myself, and I got a job as a bookeeper for a paper-box firm. And the firm, they had a—you know, bookkeeper, stenographer, those days, were men. No women. And then I did a single for a very short time, as a hoofer. And then I met a fella by the name of Bradley, and it was 'Bradley and Kane' for about fourteen years."

"Long time," Brendan says.

"Yeah. Started with Bradley when I was about nineteen, somewhere in there. I got married, I wasn't quite twenty-one. I was married in August, nineteen fifteen." He stops, glances up the beach toward the tall steel structure of the Coney Island parachute jump, closed down years ago because it was too dangerous, but never torn down. "And I was married forty-one years. To Bobby's mother."

His voice breaks when he says it. He stands there in the bright sun, adjusting his glasses, looking straight up the beach. He looks small and alone.

"Would you like to sit down on a bench?" I ask.

He shakes his head, doesn't look at me.

"That sun is pretty strong," Brendan says.

He shakes his head.

"Maybe we should sit down for a little while," I tell him.

He starts walking again, staring straight ahead. "Started with Bradley when I was about nineteen, yeah. We went with a burlesque show. We did a blackface comedy act. Comedy, singing—those years, you had to do everything." He seems to brighten with that memory, turns to me, smiles, gestures with his hands. "If you got a job in a show and they wanted you to do another part, if they needed a Mick, well, they said, 'Can you do Irish?' " Now he breaks into an excellent imitation of an Irish brogue: "And you'd say, 'Ah, sure, y'know I can, m'lad, I'll be there if y'need me.' "

Brendan tries to keep him going: "When did you start traveling the circuits?"

"We went over the Sullivan-Considine circuit when I was —uh—let's see. About twenty, I think. Al Jolson, Jimmy Wall, Arthur Rigby, we were all blackface comedians. Bradley and I got a hundred and a quarter for the team, Al Jolson got sixty dollars, single. We were getting more money each than Jolson. And we were all friends. Jimmy Wall—all minstrel men."

We walk along in silence for a while.

"Did the act change as you went along?" Brendan asks.

"Listen, you didn't change. For years. The Keith office had three hundred and seventy theaters. Booking, they were all *week*-stands. The Loews circuit, they started that split-week business. Three and four shows a day. Before that, you did two shows a day and that was it. You did a matinee performance and an evening performance and that was it."

Three young girls jog toward us, wearing tight T-shirts and very short cutoffs. Harry's head turns as they pass us, eyes following every move. Now he glances at me, adjusts his glasses, and we both laugh softly.

"Something, huh?" he says.

"Now I know why you take walks every day."

"Things like that keep up my *interest.* "

I laugh, look at his eyes, laugh again.

"And that's not *all,* " he says, timing it just right.

"Eighty-seven years old," Brendan says.

"Listen, don't let the numbers fool you." He breaks into his fine Irish brogue: "It's all accordin' to how y'feel, y'know. Sure, if the good Lord had wanted us Schenectady lads to keep it down at eighty-seven years of age—why, he'd of splashed some water on the fire, now, wouldn't y'think? Ah, but the good Lord takes care of his own, don't he? Let's sit down and cool it a bit, what d'ya say to that?"

We cross to the ocean side of the boardwalk, glancing at each other, then we have to walk about fifty yards more before we can find an empty bench. The metal railing overlooking the beach is on a section of the boardwalk that's been repaired, a long section with new tan-colored boards. The next section, to our right, has the old black boards, followed by another new section, then an old one, the widest of all, in front of the food and drink stands. When you look down between the slats, sometimes you see groups of kids in the sand below, sitting in the shade.

We finally find an empty bench and sit down, Harry at one end, Brendan in the middle, plenty of room for all of us. The wood is warm. I take out a pack of cigars, offer Harry one; he refuses with a wave of his hand. There's a pause and he looks at us and smiles a bit stiffly, as if he knows what's coming and understands we have to discuss it. Good view of the beach and sea through the railing. We hear music from a portable radio somewhere nearby and the sound of distant voices.

I light my cigar. "Want to talk about it?"

"Why not?" He squints at the sea. "Ron and I were always very close. See, when he was a kid, a teenager, Bobby was always on the road, so over those years I was like a father to him. And he was a good kid, too, basically. Oh, I mean, he'd get in the usual scrapes. You know boys that age. And he'd always come to me when he was in a jam. And I'd try to be strict with him and give him sound advice, but I'd always try and help him out. Whatever it was, money, advice, I was always there. You know how it is with kids, you love 'em but you try not to spoil 'em. Easier said than done."

"I know exactly what you mean," I say. "I've got a son of my own."

He smiles. "Yeah? Easier said than done, right?"

"I'm learning that."

"Mr. Laslo," Brendan says softly. "Did you have a fairly long talk with him today?"

"No. Half an hour, something like that. He's a—in my opinion, he's a scared kid. Scared and confused."

"What makes you think so?" I ask.

"The way he acts, the way he talks. I mean, Leslie and I, we hadn't seen him in—I don't know, maybe two months. He didn't even call in all that time, which was very unusual. Now he shows up at the apartment this afternoon straight out of the blue. Says he wants to borrow a large suitcase, that he's going on a trip. Actually apologized to us for asking. He says he priced the big suitcases up on the avenue, but they were too expensive."

"What avenue?" Brendan asks.

"Brighton Beach Avenue, the main drag. I says, 'Ron, do you need money?' He says, 'No, thanks.' I says, 'How in hell're you going on a trip if you don't even have enough money to buy a suitcase?' He tells us he's expecting some money soon, then he'll leave town. I tried to talk some sense into him. I sat him down, I says, 'Look,' I says. 'You're only thirty-six years old, you're still a young man.' I told him, I says, 'I could get you a good lawyer, you could give yourself up, let him cop a plea for you.' He says, 'Grandpa, you don't understand, I killed one of those girls.' He says, 'I didn't mean to, I swear to God, I didn't mean to, but I killed her.' I says, 'It don't matter, it was an accident, things like this happen all the time.' I says, 'You could plead involuntary manslaughter, you could get off with maybe ten, fifteen years.' I says, 'You were a good cop before, you had an excellent record, you had fourteen commendations in fourteen years.' I told him, I says, 'All that will be taken into consideration when the time comes.' He says, 'You don't understand, Grandpa, it's more complicated than that.' I says, 'What's to understand?' I says, 'What's so complicated?' I says, 'Let me tell you something that maybe *you* don't understand.' I told him the truth, I says, 'Ron, your mom and dad, you're breaking their hearts, you're breaking *our* hearts.' I says, 'We all love you, we'll always love you, we want to help you, we want you to do the right thing.' He says, 'I love you, too, all of you, but I can't do it. I can't give myself up now, it's too late.' What the hell's he mean, it's too late?"

I study my cigar, flick the ashes carefully. "Mr. Laslo, do you know where Ron is now?"

He hesitates for just an instant. "No. But what's he mean, it's too late? You understand what he means?"

"I know this," I tell him. "Unfortunately, Ron's in more serious trouble than he's told you."

"What's he done now?"

"You'll find out sooner or later, so I might just as well tell you now. He's holding a policewoman hostage and demanding a ransom for her. Says he'll kill her unless he gets half a million dollars by tomorrow morning."

The old man blinks at me, his eyes magnified behind the thick glasses. "Oh, no. Oh, my God."

"That's what he wanted the suitcase for. The money."

He squints at the beach, shakes his head slowly. "A policewoman. And he—did he actually say he'd kill her?"

"Mr. Laslo," Brendan says quietly. "We've talked to him on the phone, last night and this morning. And he let us talk to the policewoman this morning, so we could be sure she was still alive. There's no doubt in our minds that he'll kill her if anything goes wrong. He'll kill her and then kill himself. He's told us that. He means it. Ron's a very sick man. I'm sure you know that. He needs help."

Harry nods, his bald head beaded with sweat now. "Suppose—just suppose—I knew where the boy was. And suppose I told you. What guarantee would I have that you wouldn't hurt him real bad or kill him?"

I lean forward, look him in the eye. "I'd give you my

personal guarantee that we'd do our very best not to hurt him.
And certainly not to kill him. The last thing we want to do
is kill the man."

"Would you promise me something?"

I shrug. "Depends on what you ask."

"I want you to promise that you won't kill the boy."

"I'll promise you this: I'll promise that the man who's in
charge of this operation, Chief of Detectives Vadney, will issue
an official order to take him alive and unharmed if at all
possible. I can promise you that. And I'll personally do everything I can do to make sure that order is carried out."

He frowns, looks at the sea. His eyes fill quickly then and
he removes his glasses to wipe them with a handkerchief. Now
he continues to gaze at the sea. I'm just about to say something
when he smiles, a gentle smile, as if he's seen an old friend,
and his voice is soft and warm: "When Bobby was fourteen,
we were practically broke. We had fighting to do then, fighting
to get booking. He was neither child nor grownup. And it was
tough getting work. Because he outgrew the baby business.
And he wasn't old enough to be on his own and travel on his
own. We were living at a place called the Hotel America,
corner of Neptune and Stillwell in Coney Island, just north of
the amusement park. This was in nineteen thirty-one and
things were very bad. I remember, there were these kids from
Pittsburgh, a set band, and they were stranded. They were on
the breadline and we took them in, we took them to this Hotel
America with us. And, oh, were we broke. And they were
broke. And we had the one room. And they used to come up,
and they hadn't eaten, and I used to get a few bucks and go
over to—corner of Surf and Cropsey. They had markets below
the El there. They had markets on the street there—pushcarts,
y'know? And I used to buy eggs, about ten or twelve cents a
dozen, and a loaf of bread." He laughed to himself. "Get back
to the hotel. We had a one-burner thing, y'know? And I used
to fry eggs on there and feed the whole bunch and ourselves

as well. No, we had rough times and good times, y'know. As he got older, we kept using up what we had, and pretty soon we had nothing left. But that was all—that was all a long time ago, when we were very young. And very happy."

I wait a while. Then: "Mr. Laslo, is Ron in that hotel?"

He nods, still looking at the sea. He's very moved. "Don't know which room. Please try not to hurt him. Keep your promise."

"You can depend on it."

Back to the Brighton Beach BMT station, take the train west to the next and last station, Coney Island, we figure we'll call the chief from there. Haven't been out this way in years, I'm enjoying the view from the elevated tracks. To be accurate, this whole strip of south Brooklyn, from Oriental Beach on the east end to Seagate on the west, including Brighton Beach and Manhattan Beach, is all technically Coney Island, although today most New Yorkers only refer to the area around the amusement park by that name. It's not really an island, most of the middle of it is connected to the mainland. My father took me to Coney Island sometime in 1939 when I was almost seven years old. Don't remember too much about the trip except for the parachute jump, the roller coaster, and the huge Ferris wheel, but I still have the official souvenir booklet, and it gives an interesting thumbnail sketch of the area's history. Like, in Dutch times, it was just a seven-mile-long sandy strip inhabited only by rabbits, so they named it Konijn Eiland (Rabbit Island). Around the early 1800s, people started tagging it with its English "sound-alike" name, Coney Island. In the 1830s, wealthy New Yorkers began visiting the un-spoiled beaches here and soon it was a fashionable resort with elegant hotels, casinos, and hippodromes. But by the 1880s, the exclusive atmosphere was gone, the rich were gone, and it gradually evolved into a large amusement park flanked by a popular beach. Today, on any hot summer Sunday, this place routinely draws 100,000 people. If you don't get out here early in the morning, forget it, the beach is a sea of bodies, and the park is a snakepit of waiting lines. Of course, now, late in October, the amusement park is closed and the beach is deserted.

Get off the train with everybody else, end of the line, walk down the stairs, head north on Stillwell Avenue toward Neptune. We're very much aware of the fact that Laslo would recognize me instantly, even from a window of the hotel (he's never seen Brendan, to our knowledge), so we discuss our strategy. Essentially, all we want to do at this point, before we call headquarters, is to get a perspective on the hotel, to determine the degree of difficulty involved in doing temporary surveillance, front and back, until Vadney and Mairs arrive with an ESD team to surround the place. Our guess, Laslo's staying in the room almost all the time to minimize the possibility of Jessica making any kind of distress signals, noises that might attract the attention of people in adjoining rooms.

When we're about half a block away, we catch a glimpse of the hotel on the northeast corner of Neptune and Stillwell. It's an ancient six-story structure with a vertical sign hanging from the corner: Hotel America. Can't see any of the windows yet, but this is as far as I go. There's a little bookstore just ahead, we agree to meet there. Now we split up, Brendan crosses to the west side of the street, removes his tie, opens his collar, takes off his blazer, slings it over his shoulder.

I go in the store, Boshnick Books, browse around, look over the new hardcover releases in fiction. New novel by Robert Daley called *The Dangerous Edge.* Happen to like this guy, read three of his previous books, two nonfiction cop stories, *Target Blue* and *Prince of the City,* both made into films, and a novel, *To Kill a Cop,* that became the TV series "Eishied." Thing about Daley, this guy knows what he's talking about. He should. He was our Deputy Police Commissioner in 1971–1972 and studied NYPD inside-out.

Less than fifteen minutes later, Brendan's back, we go outside, walk south toward the subway station. He's drawn a diagram of the hotel and taken careful notes.

"It's completely unattached," he says. "Almost like a square box. Six stories, eight windows across, two fire escapes on all four sides. Three exits, front, back, east side. There's a coffee shop directly across the street, one of us can sit at a window table. Me, because he probably goes in there for take-out orders. You'll have to cover the alley out back. If he comes out the east-side exit, he's got to go around front to reach the street, so we got him covered. I didn't go in the lobby, didn't want to risk it."

Back to the subway station, call Vadney's office. I tell Brendan he should do this, he researched the hotel, but he says I outrank him in seniority, and besides, he dreads being tape-recorded on the phone, especially when it's something important. Horrifies him to imagine how many times the Duke will play it back. Spooks the piss out of him. Stutters every time he talks about it. Me, I take it in stride. Look forward to it. Particularly when I'm the bearer of glad tidings. Figure the more he hears my voice, the more he'll be thinking about me when he's selecting special-assignment teams. Fun and games. Like playing hooky. I light up a cigar before I dial.

Doris answers. "Chief Vadney's office."

"Hey, Doris, John Rawlings."

"Hey, John, what's happening?"

"Think we located Laslo."

"No shit! Congratulations! Hold on." Click.

Short pause while the chief cleans the mess on his chair. Click. "Rawlings, y'*found* him?"

"Think so, Chief."

"*Where?*"

"Hotel America, Coney Island. Talked with his grandfather, who met with him this afternoon. Brendan cased the hotel, we'll set up surveillance until you—"

"Don't go *near* it, Little John! He's *seen* you, he *knows* you! Where you at now?"

"Coney Island subway station."

"Okay, listen up now, get this: Stay exactly where you are, the both of ya. I'll be down there with Mairs and his team in —it's four thirty-five now. Wait a minute, lemme look at this map here. Okay. Okay, we'll take the Brooklyn-Battery Tunnel, then the Gowanus, then the Prospect, then Ocean Parkway straight south to Coney. Should be there in—wait a minute, we'll hit the rush-hour traffic smack on. Fuck 'em, we'll use sirens, lights, the whole ESD bag. Should be there inside of an hour. Don't go *near* that hotel, Little John, neither of ya, *hear?*"

"I hear you."

"Y'*read* me, buddy-boy?"

"I read you."

Bang! Hangs up.

I puff my cigar, keep talking into the receiver for Brendan's benefit: "Well, thank you, Chief. Kind of you to say so. Commendations for both of us? Fantastic, we really appreciate that." I glance over at Brendan, who's standing there wide-eyed. "Just one last thing I should add, Chief. I've taken the liberty of placing your name in nomination for the coveted Horse's Ass of the Century Award. Which I'm sure you'll win moons up."

"John." Doris's voice startles me; she stayed on the line.

"Oh, shit. Sorry, Doris."

"Don't be. I already nominated him."

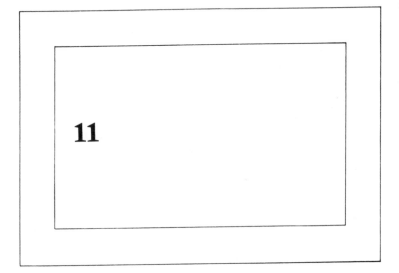

11

ONE THING ABOUT THE CHIEF, he's a consummate politician. When he arrives at the Coney Island subway station at 5:45, followed by two unmarked ESD vans (no sirens or flashing lights at this point), guess who steps out of his car to be in on the biggie action? Marty Shugrue and Dave Pearson, who, along with Jim Mairs, Jerry Grady, Brendan, and me, are the only people he's taken into his confidence about the whole hostage situation. Grady's in a different category, of course, he's here with his ever-present Nikon and strobe to record the collar for posterity, if we get it, but his role is positively essential on any list of the chief's top priorities. In any event, I'm glad to see Marty and Dave, they've both busted their humps on this case from the beginning, they deserve to be around for the glory, if that's what you'd call it. We're in the middle of rush hour, heavy traffic, crowds pouring off the subway, so the three vehicles melt into the general chaos, all parked illegally under the El, but widely separated. Brendan and I walk over to Vadney, who's leaning against his car, waiting for us with the others; none of the ESD men have left their vans. We fill the brass in on basics and Brendan shows them his diagram and notes on the hotel. Naturally, I tell the chief about my promise to Harry Laslo.

He frowns, blinks, raises his voice above the street noises. "Wait a minute, let me get this straight, Rawlings. You promised him that I'm gonna give an official *order* to that effect?"

"Yes, sir."

"That Laslo should be taken *unharmed?*"

"Unharmed, if at all possible, yes."

"Rawlings, are you fuckin' crazy?"

"It was the only way he'd give us the information, Chief. It was the key. Without that promise, we wouldn't be here."

He shrugs, turns to Mairs. "Yeah, well, consider the order given, for what it's worth, tell your men." Then, to me: "Like I said from the start, I intend to collar this fucker personally, Little John, and I can't imagine him goin' the easy way."

Mairs takes Brendan's diagram and notes. "First things first. I'll meet with my men—I've got ten—and work out a strategy to occupy whatever surrounding buildings we can. John, is the hotel within easy walking distance from here?"

"Yeah. Just up Stillwell there to Neptune."

"All right. We'll go up side streets, enter side entrances whenever possible, see what's what. I'll send them one by one, well staggered, have them radio back." He glances up at the sky. "With any luck, we should have everybody in place before dark."

And he does. By 6:25, in deepening twilight, Mairs has his men positioned in windows and/or roofs of five buildings with excellent views of all four sides of the Hotel America. Each of these ten officers is a sharpshooter armed with a high-powered rifle, each has a photo of Laslo, each has binoculars, each has a walkie-talkie, and each has been instructed to take extra-special precautions not to be seen, on the very realistic assumption that, given Laslo's experience and predictable paranoia, he might routinely scan the windows of all buildings within his view. If only one glint of one officer's rifle barrel is seen, even for a split-second, it could be the end. Every man understands that fact.

Our basic strategy is simple: Sit tight and wait. Wait for Laslo to exit the hotel for food, drink, newspapers, anything. If and when he does, no matter what time, Vadney has first crack at him. And where will the chief hide? Precisely where Laslo would never, ever, suspect him to be, thanks to the almost incredible ingenuity of Jim Mairs, who just seems to have a God-given gift for imaginative—some would say bizarre—surveillance techniques. Jim takes one quick peek at the hotel from the roof of the apartment building above the coffee shop that's directly across the street and—*bingo!*—it hits him. Now he goes down, finds a pay phone, calls his buddy Jeff Kennedy, night supervisor for gas and steam emergencies at Con Ed, 4 Irving Place, 683-8830. Asks Kennedy for a rundown on the Con Ed underground conduits leading to the manhole at Neptune and Stillwell. Kennedy checks the system map, tells him that particular conduit can be entered from the Con Ed manhole at the corner of Neptune and Cropsey, which is the closest, just two blocks west. Mairs explains what we want to do, gets permission, he's done it before.

In all the turmoil of getting his team together and rushing to Coney Island, Chief understandably neglected to notify the command of jurisdiction, the Sixtieth Precinct, 2951 West Eighth Street, Brooklyn. Now he gets on the pay phone, calls the Sixtieth, speaks to Commander Bill Boggs, tells him the basics and locale, asks him to order patrol units out of the vicinity until further notice. Boggs agrees.

Chief tells Brendan and me to accompany Mairs and him back to the subway station, we need special ESD equipment from the vans. Soon as we get close, we notice three things. One: Chief's car is missing; two: a commercial towtruck is hooking up one of the vans; three: an NYPD squad car is parked nearby and two uniformed officers are standing there giving orders. Chief goes instantly nuts, sprints away from us, crosses the street just as the traffic light changes. Traffic's much too heavy for us to cross, but we can see and hear clearly.

"You fuckin' assholes!" Chief shouts.

The younger cop, a tall, skinny kid, yells back: "Watcha mouth, ya piece a slime! This ya van heah?"

"I'm Chief Vadney!"

"Yeah, an I'm Ed Koch! Y'under arrest! Up against the van!"

"Are you fuckin' *crazy!*"

Kid grabs him, slams him against the van. "Spread ya legs! Y'under arrest heah! Impoysinatin' a police officer!"

It's all happening so fast, cars and trucks whizzing past, we can't believe it. Of course, we could all yell across at the cops and waive our gold, shit like that, but we don't. Actually, at this point in time, we can't. We're laughing too hard. Mairs's fault, he's the one started it, he's bent over now, breaking up. Brendan and me, we're not really what you'd call laughing out loud, we're standing there with these, well, grins, you might say, making these, well, sounds deep in our throats, like barks and growls. Sounds to that effect. Soon as the light changes, we all get deadpan serious in a hurry, run across, all holding out our gold and shouting, "Police officers!"

Both cops give us the classic double-take, then go wide-eyed on Vadney, who turns around and finally manages to pull his gold.

"Oh, my Gawd," young cop says.

"Holy jumped-up Jesus," older cop says.

"Where the fuck's my *car?*" Chief demands.

Young cop blinks rapidly. "Ya kaw, sir?"

"Dark-blue Ford Fairmont, 'eighty-three!"

"Dark-blue Ford Fair—? Oh, my Gawd."

Towtruck driver knows his cue: "I yanked it about ten minutes ago, sir. On orders from these here officers."

Chief stands tall, sticks out his big right forefinger, stubs it rhythmically against the young cop's chest, punctuating each word: "What! Is! Your! Name!"

"Patrolman Angelo Rizzutti, sir."

"Who! Is! Your! Commanding! Officer!"

"Commander William Boggs, sir."

Chief removes his finger. "Rizzuto, I want that—"

"Rizzutti, sir."

"—car back in exactly—*what?!*"

"Nothin', sir."

"Has it sunk in who you're *talkin'* to, Rizzuto?"

"Chief of Police Vadney, sir."

"Chief of—?! Chief of *Detectives* Vadney, ya fuckin' numskull! Chief of *Detectives* Vadney, who you had the arrogance to call a *slimebag!* Right?"

"No, sir. I didn't do no such thing."

"Ya did too! I *heard* ya!"

"No, sir. My exact woids, sir, I called ya 'a *piece* a slime,' sir. I got my pawtnah Nunzio heah as a witness, right, Nunzio?"

Nunzio closes his eyes at the horror of it all, but nods.

Rizzutti nods. "Yeah, but see, at that point in time, Nunzio and me didn't know who we was tawkin' to, sir."

"Well, now you know!"

"Yeah, sir. But, beggin' ya pardon, Chief, we had provocation, y'know? I mean, ya up an called Nunzio an me fuckin' assholes foist."

Chief clenches his fists by his sides. "Rizzuto, if I don't get that fuckin' car back here inside a fifteen minutes, y'know what I'm gonna do to yer ass?"

"No, sir, but this heah ain't my fawlt, sir."

"*What?!*"

"Beggin' y'pardon, sir, but Nunzio an me, we was just doin'

our reglah job heah, followin' the book, y'know?"

He's right, of course. He knows he's right, we all know he's right. Young, arrogant, stubborn, but dead right. Stands right up to the chief, looks him in the eye, refuses to back down. I'm watching this kid, I can't help but think of when I started out as a patrolman in the Bushwick section of Brooklyn back in 1955. Truth is, I never would've talked to the Chief of Detectives like this guy, right or wrong, I had too much respect for the brass. Three years and four citations later, I got recommended for a plainclothes job. Different world back then. Wonder how far this kid will go with his attitude.

Now something interesting happens. Chief cools down, tries the diplomatic approach. Explains we're in an emergency situation at Neptune and Stillwell, tells him Commander Boggs is ordering all units out of the immediate vicinity. Kid responds like a veteran, all business now, tells the towtruck driver to unhook the van immediately, says he'll personally drive Vadney's car back as soon as possible. Salutes and takes off with his partner. Like I said before, Chief's a mixed metaphor, classic schizophrenic, one extreme to the other, but you got to hand it to him, you got to admit one overwhelming truth about him that somehow makes up for a multitude of sins: This fucker is never boring.

Mairs leads us to the second van, we all climb in, sit in back while he explains his game plan in detail and the special equipment we'll need. I say "we" because Vadney, Brendan, and me are going to work eight-hour surveillance shifts around the clock. From where? Knew you'd ask. From inside the manhole in front of the hotel. Yeah! Don't go away, it gets better. Chief thinks this is the most ingenious surveillance idea he's ever heard. And this is the guy who calls Mairs "Commander Cuckoo" behind his back. Naturally, we need fashionable attire for such a gala evening, so we strip down to essentials while Mairs acts as valet. ESD vans are positive masterpieces of compartmentalized paraphernalia with sophisticated high-tech gear guaranteed to make your standard career criminal drool with envy.

What are the latest tony togs for that exotic Cop-in-the-Manhole look these crisp autumn evenings? Head to toe, get this: Tonight we have our macho adjustable hardhat in nonreflective black; our designer lightweight bulletproof vest in matching black, worn under our figure-flattering black cotton jumpsuit with wide black leather belt for chic accessories like black-holstered guns and walkie-talkies, black infrared nightscopes and black flashlights, black handcuffs and heavy-duty crowbars; a light touch is provided by our high-camp skintight black leather gloves; our exclusive high black sneakers add just the right pinch of punk (mine are about two sizes too big, which is even punkier); finally, Mairs has to blacken our faces and necks—every inch—with some special commando nonreflective makeup, yet. Wind up looking like Harry Laslo's blackface comedians. Feel like doing a fast buck-and-wing, except I'd trip over my turned-up sneakers. Have this irresistible urge to get down on my knees, spread my arms, and sing: *"I'd walk a million blocks/ For ya bagels and lox,/My dear ol' Maaa-hah-hah-meee!"*

Now the fun begins. We sit in back out of sight while Mairs drives west on Surf, hangs a right, heads north on Cropsey to Neptune. Have to admit it, every time I glance at Vadney, it's all I can do to keep from breaking up. I mean, the lights are out now, all I can see of his face are the whites of his eyes and the occasional glint of a tooth. We've been working since early morning and it's now 7:20 and all of us are tired and hungry. Me, I'm beginning to feel a bit lightheaded and silly. Think what I need more than anything else at this point is a couple of fast and dry Beefeater martinis on the rocks with a twist. Given that, I'm sure this whole operation would be transformed into something elemental and profound. Laughable, but profound, too.

Mairs explains basic logistics as he drives: "Getting the manhole cover off is no sweat, I've done it before. One end of these crowbars fits the top niche perfectly, then you just apply leverage to pry it off initially. But it's heavy iron, we'll need all our crowbars to get it completely off. Now, there's a permanent steel ladder attached to one side of the hole. The ladder extends down to two levels with passages at each level. Level one contains the big main Con Ed steam and gas pipes and extends the entire length of Neptune. That's about fifty feet below street level and that's the one you'll use. It's just a two-block walk through the passage, the tunnel. The next ladder extends up to the manhole at Neptune and Stillwell, almost directly in front of the hotel. You climb the ladder, use a crowbar to pry open the cover and get your bearings. Then you have two options: You can leave the cover open a crack by bracing it with a crowbar, which would give you a constant view of the hotel's entrance, or you can close the cover, climb down to level one and wait, maintaining frequent radio contact. Frankly, I'd recommend the first option. It's harder, you'll have to stand on the ladder, or sit on it with your legs braced against the side, but you'll be right up there, ready to go on an instant's notice when the call comes, when Laslo exits the hotel."

"What're the disadvantages?" Chief asks.

"Traffic banging over the manhole cover. Still, this time of night, maybe another hour or so, traffic should be minimal. I don't believe it's a serious consideration compared to the obvious advantages. Also, it'll give you better ventilation."

"What's at the second level down?" Brendan asks.

Mairs chooses his words carefully. "The main sewer conduit. But that's a total of seventy-five feet below street level."

"Is it *open* down there?" Chief asks.

"There's an opening, of course, but it's very small, the same diameter as the manhole cover."

Chief's white eyes get bigger. "Jim, let me get this straight, we didn't discuss this. Are you sayin' there's raw sewage rushin' past the opening down there?"

"Yes, but that's a good twenty-five feet below you. The

ladder extends down into an enormous conduit down there, a huge tunnel."

"*Raw sewage* floatin' past?" Chief asks.

"Certainly."

"Shouldn't we wear gas masks or somethin'?"

"Sure, if you want 'em, no problem."

Corner of Neptune and Cropsey, Mairs double-parks the van, comes back, snaps on the lights, gets out three modern-looking black gas masks: Lightweight facepiece with aviator-style lenses and an outlet valve connected to a small canister. He fits them on us himself, trying not to smudge the black makeup. Now we put on our black hardhats, check to see if we have all our gear.

Exactly 7:35, we file out the rear of the van. Street's well lighted, stores closed, traffic's very light, only a few pedestrians. Manhole is located on the north side of Neptune, not the middle. We go to work fast, Mairs starts us off, fits the end of his crowbar into the niche on the cover, applies leverage, maneuvers the cover off a few inches, just enough for the three of us to hook our crowbars under and drag it completely off the hole. Look around, a couple of pedestrians are gawking, as well they might, we look totally weird. Mairs flashes his gold, tells them it's a police emergency, asks them to leave the area immediately. They do. Chief says he'll go down first. Brendan and I snap on our flashlights, direct the beams onto the steel ladder at the side. Chief climbs down slowly, reaches level one in less than thirty seconds. Brendan goes next. A car drives past very, very slowly, predictable gawks; Mairs shows his gold, tells them to leave fast.

He turns to me. "I'll send food down as soon as you get settled. Sandwiches, coffee, anything you want. Just get on the radio."

"Beefeater martini on the rocks. Very dry."

He smiles. "Why the hell not?"

"Coffee cup with my name on the lid."

"You got it."

Brendan's down, steps off the ladder, now he and Vadney play their flashlight beams up the shaft for me. Looks like a long way down.

"Make it a double," I tell Jim.

"*Big* coffee cup. Twist?"

"Please. Pay you later."

"Expense account. Hazardous duty."

Stick my flashlight and crowbar in the holders on my belt, take a deep breath, down I go. Ever try climbing down a narrow ladder in sneakers two sizes too large? Inspires confidence. Thought suddenly hits me, if I slip and fall, I'll sail straight through the openings at both levels and plunge into a raging river of shit. What a way to go. Wonder who'd have the nose to look for me? Hang on a bit tighter now, go a bit slower. Success. Step off the ladder onto solid steel, nice feeling, grab my flashlight. No small-talk, Chief leads the way, Brendan behind him. Relatively wide steel tunnel with two huge pipes down the center. Chief's flashlight beam extends far into the distance, tunnel seems endless, narrows to a vanishing point. Warm down here. Eerie. Only one sound, fairly loud too, relentless: Rushing water from level two. Even feel the vibrations. Horrible question crosses my mind: What would happen if, by sheer chance, everybody in every bathroom on Coney Island flushes their toilets simultaneously? My guess, every manhole cover on the island gets blown into the wild blue yonder. Hundreds of gushers twenty stories high, black gold. Talk about acid rain? Rowboats in the streets for weeks. Bulldozers for months. Gas masks for years.

Takes us ten long minutes to walk the two blocks. Our shadows move long and grotesque along the top and sides of the tunnel. Chief creature finally reaches the ladder on the manhole leading up to Neptune and Stillwell. Shines his beam up the shaft to the cover fifty feet above us. Snaps off his light, tells us in his distorted gas-mask voice to play our beams on the ladder and shaft as he climbs up. We do. Up he goes, shadow like a giant grasshopper. Standing here at the edge of the shaft, the abyss, the raging river below is much louder, of course, and the vibrations stronger. Half a minute later, Chief reaches the top, pulls the crowbar off his belt, pries the lid up about an inch, braces it by sliding an end of the crowbar under it. Now he takes a long look around. Giggles through his gas mask, must like what he sees. Suddenly—*BLAM!-BANG!-BLAM!*—somebody drives over the manhole. Now the heavy iron lid wobbles around like a big coin up there. Chief's holding the top of his hardhat, lid must've conked him good. Distorted gasmask voice seems to be saying: *"Yagoddamsonofamotherfuckinassholepigfucker!"* Words to that effect.

Finally, he lifts his gas mask and calls down to us: "I'll take the first shift! Radio out for food and coffee! Tell 'em we're all set!"

Brendan gets out his walkie-talkie, calls Jim Mairs, gets an immediate reply; he's waiting in the van at Neptune and Cropsey. Brendan tells him all systems are go, Chief's set to lift-off. Now, orders: Chief's all-time favorite foot-long hero sandwich, jammed with everything they got, on a soft sesame-seed roll; for us antiheroes, two cheeseburgers each, medium-rare, pickles, chopped fried onions, ketchup and mustard, soft sesame-seed buns, plus a couple sides of fries, extra ketchup, please; three large coffees, cream and sugar on the side; lots of napkins for the hero, we've seen how those suckers ooze when held in the Duke's big mitts.

Now all we can do is sit tight and wait. Brendan braces his flashlight up against the ladder so the beam shines up the shaft but not directly in the chief-creature's face. Before we move back from the abyss, I play my light straight down the shaft into the second-level conduit and the sight surprises me. From what I can see of the tunnel down there, it's so enormous that the raging river looks more like a fast-flowing creek. Deceptive. Probably deep. One could like walk along the, uh, "shore" down there. If one cared to. Reminds me of a story. Tell you later.

Brendan and I sit back now, my flashlight between us, glance at each other, chuckle despite ourselves. Now look at the fine mess you've gotten us into. Irony is, we could easily have avoided it and still obtained the creative surveillance advantages. Mairs's original idea, long before this one, was to call his buddy at Con Ed, have him send over an emergency crew, set up their truck and equipment around the manhole in front of the hotel, then go down in and "create" a steam-leak emergency, complete with real steam. That way, Vadney, in a clean white Con Ed uniform, hardhat, safety glasses, maybe even a gas mask, could've sat in the truck and waited in relative comfort. No way, Chief wouldn't buy the idea. Reason? Thinks Lalso might possibly anticipate such a routine. If he was outside the hotel, he'd never go near it; if he was inside, he'd be on the pay phone fast, threatening to kill Jessica. Me, I don't happen to believe such a routine is obvious at all. I've been around twenty-eight years, exactly twice as long as Laslo, and I only know of maybe half a dozen times we've used this particular type of camouflage, even in terrorist situations. Why? First and foremost, we'd be endangering the lives of the Con Ed workers, or the employees of any other commercial outfit. So I don't happen to agree with the chief. But then, I'm not as paranoid as either Vadney or Laslo. So here we sit. Probable all-night vigil inside a manhole.

BLAM!-BANG!-BLAM! Wobble-wobble-wobble! "*Yagoddamsonofabitchincornholer!*"

"Brendan," I say in my Boris Karloff gas-mask voice. "Ever read those stories about life in the New York City sewer system?"

"*Life* in the sewer system? No."

"Documented stories, in all the papers some years back. TV news, too. Never heard about it?"

"Can't recall it, John. What?"

"Well, some years back . . . Naw. Naw, too horrible. Tell you some other time."

"No, go ahead, John. You know me, I don't scare easy."

"Well, some years back, nineteen fifty-six, as I recall, long before you joined the department—"

"Hell, I was still in Wicklow, Ireland, in 'fifty-six. Didn't come over till 'fifty-seven."

"Yeah, that's right, forgot that. Anyhow, I'll give you a very brief background. Seems like throughout the years, a variety of wild creatures have been flushed into the New York sewer system and managed to survive in the tunnels down there. Eyewitness accounts of sewer maintenance workers confirmed large families of alligators, crocodiles, squid, lizards, snakes, turtles, in addition to the expected colonies of rats, mice, bats, spiders, cockroaches, and so on. Apparently, conditions are ideal. In the wet, warm, dark, isolated atmosphere of main sewer tunnels, some of these creatures have grown to abnormal sizes and produced weird mutations of their species."

"How the hell did alligators and crocodiles get in there?"

"Easy. People buy 'em as tiny baby pets, they start growing, too dangerous for the kids, so they flush 'em."

"Never knew that."

"Yeah. So here's the story. In May of that year, 'fifty-six, buildings on Eighth Avenue between Forty-second and Fifty-ninth streets experience plumbing troubles. Twelve-man crew of sewer maintenance workers is assigned an exploratory check for possible blockage of tributory pipes leading into Tunnel Twenty-seven, the principal sewage conduit below Eighth Avenue. As the crew's working, they discover the mutilated body of a young man who's hanging by his right wrist from a handcuff locked to a steel ring in the side of Tunnel Twenty-seven. His legs and abdomen have been eaten away and the remainder of his body is crawling with various rodents who're finishing the job. After cutting the handcuff, the crew brings the body to street level, where it's transported to the office of the chief medical examiner. An autopsy determines that the kid was approximately seventeen years old. Apparently, he was cuffed to the tunnel while he was alive. In an attempt to escape, he tried to chew his right hand off at the wrist."

Brendan looks at me through his gas-mask goggles. "John, maybe you're right, maybe you should save this for a more— appropriate time and place, y'know?"

"Thought you didn't scare easy."

"Me? I don't. No way. Go ahead."

"Subsequent to the autopsy, a routine check of fingerprints produces a positive ID. Victim was a known male prostitute and junkie who had an arrest record dating back two years. Within a couple of weeks, an exhaustive search of Tunnel Twenty-seven uncovers the skeletal remains of seven other bodies, each hanging from a handcuff on the right wrist, each a teenaged male. Positive identifications are impossible."

"John, we're gonna have dinner here in a little while, huh?"

I pause, listen to the rushing water, then continue. "So, clearly, a madman is at work, probably selecting victims from the ten-block stretch of Eighth Avenue that was then known as the Minnesota Strip, peopled primarily by kids. Back then, at night, the sidewalks are always jammed with thousands of teenage runaways, castoffs, nomads, and derelicts. About three-quarters of 'em are hookers—far more boys than girls— and roughly half are from New York. Saturation press coverage of the murders results in an atmosphere of real anxiety among the entire population of the Strip."

"Anxiety? Must've been closer to panic."

"Yeah. Lots of real scared kids. One of 'em to emerge was a kid named Nick Castiglione, a nineteen-year-old con artist and drug-pusher who'd been on his own since the age of thirteen. He comes into it later. By mid-June, two more bodies are discovered in Tunnel Twenty-seven, both recently killed, same MO as the eight others, bodies intact enough for autopsy and positive ID by fingerprints. Both were teenage males, known hookers and dealers who lived in the Reno Hotel on West Forty-sixth Street, just off the Strip. Now, Nick Castiglione, who also lives in that hotel, is finally scared enough to approach a cop who's busted him several times, Lieutenant Charley Donehue of Midtown North. Tough, bright, fifty-two-year-old veteran who's seen it all in thirty-one years in the department. Castiglione tells him he's real scared and asks for protection. Donehue agrees to keep an eye on him in return for information. Turns out—"

BLAM!-BANG!-BLAM! Wobble-wobble-wobble! No remarks from above. I get up, walk to the ladder, glance up. Chief creature's in a sitting position, one rung lower than he was, feet braced against the side. Can't fool this guy three times. Catches on in a hurry.

Now I go back and sit down. "Turns out Castiglione becomes an excellent informant because he's so scared. First week in July, our man Donehue puts all the pieces together, tracks down the mad killer."

We sit there, look at the weird shadows around us, listen to the rushing water.

"John. Please. Bottom *line,* huh?"

"Killer turns out to be Nick Castiglione. Didn't even know it himself until Donehue managed to trap him in the act down in Tunnel Twenty-seven. Suffered from the classic definition of multiple personality. Had three distinct, independent personalities.

"Jesus." Brendan shakes his head. "Frightening."

"Not bad for a seven-year-old kid, huh?"

"*What?*"

"Yeah. My son John. One of three short 'books' he's written, complete with color drawings. This one, he calls this book *Madman of the Sewer.*"

"Ah, Jesus. Ah, Johnny, ya dirty rotten rat, ya."

"Twenty-two pages this time. Other two books, called *Ghosts* and *Monsters,* they were shorter, not quite as imaginative."

"Ah, Jesus. Ya dirty rat, ya."

"I mean, I added a few things in the telling, his vocabulary's not that big yet, but the story's all his. Drawings are real good, too. Gifted kid. All his teachers say so."

"Where's he get such *ideas?*"

"This one, we saw a TV program called *Fact or Fiction?* Told about all the rumors over the years that all these creatures had been flushed into the New York sewer system and survived down there. Which, I'd heard the rumors too, I'd often wondered myself. So now they do the whole nine yards, they take cameras down in the sewers—this is all courtesy of the NYC Department of Environmental Protection—they interview long-time sewer maintenance workers, they interview a veteran sewer foreman, the whole shot. Turns out the rumors are absolutely false. Total bullshit. Not one of these workers has ever seen anything but occasional rats and mice down there. Anyhow, that's how John comes up with his basic idea for the story. Kid's got an imagination you wouldn't believe. Reads all the time, too. Loves mystery stories."

"Seven years old. Amazing."

"Yeah, well, he'll be eight in December, but still."

Goes like so. That's something you learn to do in surveillance duty: You learn to keep talking. You keep talking to stay alert. If it's night duty and you're tired, like us, you keep talking just to stay awake. You talk about anything at all, the wife, the kids, the mortgage, anything. You ask each other questions, you tell jokes, you debate issues, and it's important, it's critical.

Now it's just about 8:20, we're starved, looking forward to dinner, which should arrive soon, Brendan's telling me about his wife Margaret's cooking, when Marty Shugrue's voice blasts over our walkie-talkies:

"Chief, Chief! Laslo just walked out the front door!"

12

CHIEF EXPLODES from the manhole, I scramble up the ladder, adrenaline pumping like crazy, Brendan right on my heels, before I reach the top I hear Vadney yell, "Police!—Halt!" *BLAM!—BLAM!* By the time I'm up in the street, Chief's chasing Laslo south on Stillwell, top speed, middle of the street, followed by Marty Shugrue, who was in the coffee shop. I yank off my hardhat and gas mask as I run, I can see Laslo in the distance sprinting like a track star, he's opened up a big lead now, maybe half a block, he's getting close to the elevated on Surf. Chief can't fire with any accuracy, of course, same with Shugrue, he wouldn't risk it with Vadney up ahead anyhow. Don't know how many men are behind Brendan, but I'm guessing plenty. Now Laslo crosses Surf and suddenly, KA-*BOOM!*—KA-*BOOM!*, shotgun blasts, I duck automatically, keep running in a crouch, what the hell's happening? Now I see: Laslo's stopped, he's got his hands over his head, two uniformed officers with shotguns are running up to him. Guess who? Right the first time: Tall, skinny, young, arrogant

Patrolman Angelo Rizzutti and his sidekick Nunzio What's-his-name, never did find out. Now here comes Vadney. Of course, neither officer knows who this big, hardhatted, gas-masked study in black is, running toward them with a nickel-plated revolver, so Rizzutti reacts instinctively, levels his shotgun at him.

"*Hawlt!*" he yells. "*Police! Drop ya gun!*"

Chief holsters his revolver, walks the last few yards, yanks off his hardhat and gas mask. Face is completely black, he's gasping for breath, he can't even speak yet.

"I said *hawlt,* ya weird fuck, ya! Hawlt or I blow ya away!"

Fortunately, Marty Shugrue arrives now, he's waving his gold: "*Police officers! Hold your fire!*"

Rizzutti lowers his shotgun, looks Vadney up and down like maybe he's something that just crawled out of a sewer, still doesn't recognize him. I'm on the scene now, I'm so pooped I can hardly get a word out; Brendan's in next. Rizzutti and Nunzio have long since cuffed and disarmed Laslo, who stands there quietly, almost placidly, tall, trim, handsome as ever, wearing a dark turtleneck, faded denim jacket and jeans. Maybe it's my imagination, but the guy looks sort of relieved now. Relieved that it's finally over. Dave Pearson jogs in next, followed by three young officers from ESD with rifles. Rizzutti stays underwhelmed by all this, starts to read Laslo his rights.

"Wait a minute," Chief says, still out of breath. "I'll take care of that personally."

When he hears the voice, Rizzutti realizes for the first time who this big black dude is. "Oh, my Gawd. Chief Vadney, I didn't, uh—"

Chief goes diplomatic. "Excellent work, Rizzuto. You and your partner will receive a personal commendation from me."

"A poisonel—? Oh, Jeez, thank ya, sir."

"No, thank *you,* Rizzuto. And I'm sure I speak for all of us. You have any idea who you guys just collared here?"

"Uh, no, sir."

"You just collared Ron Laslo, the mass-rapist and killer we've all worked so hard to find."

"Oh, my *Gawd!* Nunzio, ya *heah* that?"

"So, naturally, on this particular collar, we've got to be absolutely, positively certain that we follow every legal mandate to the exact, precise letter of the law."

"*Deaf*enally, Chief."

"Now, Rizzuto, I was watchin' ya all the way, buddy-boy. Excellent judgment, warning shots, good solid police work. Now, there's just one small technicality I want to clear up in my own mind."

"*Deaf*enally, Chief."

"Now, think carefully. Before you started reading this perp his rights, did you, or did you not, inform him officially that he was under arrest and specify the nature of the suspected crime?"

Rizzutti hesitates, frowns, flashes a quick glance at his silent partner. "I, ah, I believe Nunzio heah done that, sir. It was, ah, I believe it was just after we fired them warnin' shots. Ah, ain't that right, Nunzio?"

For the second time tonight, Nunzio closes his eyes in horror. Now he shakes his head slowly, negatively.

Chief's eyes and left molars flash white as snow. Turns to the suspect, clears his throat. "Ronald Drake Laslo, I hereby place you under arrest on the charges of suspected rape, suspected murder, and suspected kidnapping. You have the right to remain silent. You have—"

"Forget it," Laslo says softly, head down. "She's in Room Four thirty-nine. The key's in my back pocket, right side."

Chief turns him around, reaches in his pocket, pulls out the key. "Marty, Dave, book him at the Sixtieth Precinct, let him contact an attorney immediately, hold him there till you hear from me. Listen up now: No press. Understand? Tell Commander Boggs there. No press on this collar till you hear from me."

Shugrue and Pearson take Laslo by either arm, follow Rizzutti and Nunzio to the squad car.

Chief looks like a black Persian cat who just swallowed Tweetie Pie. "Little John, Brendan, you guys come with me."

Soon as we jump in his car, he slaps the emergency lights on the roof, turns on the siren, squeals toward Stillwell, *French Connection,* blasting his horn, despite the fact there's absolutely no traffic at all. Roars up Stillwell, we're doing at least sixty when he jumps the red light at Neptune and simultaneously hangs an earsplitting, bowel-freezing right turn, skids sideways, fishtails, hooks two tires in and out of the open manhole, finally comes to a bouncing, burning, screeching stop in front of the Hotel America. Quite a crowd on the sidewalk now and virtually every window is open with gawkers hanging out. Front entrance is blocked by seven ESD officers with rifles, plus Jim Mairs who's holding three big bags with our dinners, plus Jerry Grady with his Nikon and strobe at the ready. Out we jump, three black musketeers, crowd utters a shocked collective *"Ahhhhh!"* and gives us space, more in horror than respect.

Little lobby's crowded with vocal deadbeat residents who want out. They get a load of us, they scatter fast. Tall guy at the front desk looks like Don Knotts on a bummer.

Chief flashes his gold. "Where's the elevators?"

Bug-eyed Knotts is actually shaking, stuttering, can't get the words out, he finally points to his right.

"We're goin' to four!" Chief yells. "Keep everybody off the elevators till we come down!"

Knotts nods fast, keeps nodding.

Turns out only one elevator out of the two is in service, looks like it might be fifty years old, door covered with generations of deeply scratched-on graffiti. In we go, Chief presses number four. Door creaks shut. Slowly. Machinery whirs, cables squeak. Up we go at our own risk. Slowly. Dim light. Every inch of the walls has multicolored graffiti.

Chief's black nostrils twitch. "Jesus H. Kee-ryest."

"What a dump," Brendan observes.

Chief's white eyes narrow to slits. "Some fucker *crapped* in this can!"

"Fifty years ago," I add.

Elevator bumps to a stop at four, door groans open. Dim bare gray hall reminds me of an old YMCA. Chief slaps Brendan on the shoulder, points to the right; off he goes. I follow the big black Duke to the left. Numbers begin on the left side near the elevator, odd left, even right. Hall extends around all four sides of the building. Turn right at the north end, back of the building, 439 is toward the far end on the left. As we walk quickly, soundlessly, Brendan appears at the far corner, points to the door.

Chief approaches the door cautiously, pulls his revolver, we do likewise. Brendan flattens himself against the wall to the right of the door, me against the wall to the left. Chief puts his ear to the door, listens maybe five seconds, then knocks hard.

"Police! Open up!"

Doors on both sides of the hall crack open, chain-lock secure, remain open.

"Police! Open up!"

Nothing.

Chief slips the key in the lock, *click,* turns the knob slowly, drops to a combat squat as he shoves it open fast, all the way. Room is completely dark except for a narrow band of yellow around the window shade. Chief moves inside fast, in a crouch, darts to the right to get out of the hall light. Brendan and I crouch, I signal him to wait, then move inside quickly to the left. Bed near the window holds a dark silhouette, squirming, voice making deep sounds in the throat. Chief pulls the flashlight from his belt, snaps it on and off fast, changes his position instantly. In that split-second flash of light, I see Jessica on the bed clearly, on her stomach, nude, hogtied, gagged, blindfolded.

Chief's voice is angry: "If there's anybody else in this room, give yourself up now, fast. There's no way out."

We wait. Nothing.

Chief snaps on his flashlight again, plays the beam around the room quickly. Sparsely furnished, bathroom off to my left. Keeps his light on the open bathroom door. I move toward it in a crouch, stand against the wall to the left, change gun hands, reach inside, feel for the light switch. Door is there. Must be on the other side.

"Kill it," I say quietly.

Chief snaps off his light. I wait five seconds, listen, change gun hands, then crouch and jump to the opposite side. Stand, reach inside, feel for the switch, find it, snap it on. Wait again, crouch, look around the corner. Empty, but a faded blue shower curtain is drawn around the inside of the bathtub. Only two alternatives: Go in fast and yank the curtain or throw something at it. I grab the flashlight from my belt, throw it lefty with everything I got. Whoosh-*thud-BANG!* Now I hear it rolling around on the porcelain. Music to my ears. In I go, yank the curtain back from a crouch, just to be sure. Empty. Grab my flashlight.

"All clear!" I yell.

"Brendan!" Chief shouts. "Close the door! Nobody gets in!"

Brendan comes in, takes a quick look at Jessica in the light from the bathroom, closes the door quietly from the outside. There's an overhead light in the room, but neither one of us make a move toward the switch. Chief holsters his revolver and flashlight, goes to Jessica, removes her blindfold first, then peels the two wide bands of surgical tape from her mouth, then pulls out the white handkerchief stuffed inside.

"You okay?" he asks.

Jessica coughs several times. "Yes."

"We collared him."

"Thank God."

Her wrists and ankles are tied together securely with three lengthly strands of white nylon cord. Chief looks around his belt for a knife, doesn't have one; neither do I. Although the knots are difficult to see in the dim light, he goes to work on them immediately.

I step to the open door of the little closet, snap on my flashlight. Jessica's blue windbreaker is on a hanger with her designer jeans, boots on the floor. Shelf directly above holds her white turtleneck sweater, bra, panties, socks. Nothing else in the closet. I grab her clothes, take them to the bed.

Chief's managed to untie the strand of nylon binding her wrists and ankles together, her legs are flat on the bed, now he's working on the strands around her wrists. I place her clothes on the floor, start untying her ankles. Laslo did a thorough job here, obviously took his time, four or five rows of nylon wrapped neatly around the ankles and tied with three very tight knots, then at least five rows between the ankles, just loose enough to allow circulation, but tied with knots that are extremely tight. Chief finishes first, Jessica remains on her stomach, slowly slides her arms away from each other, makes a painful sound in her throat. Thirty seconds later I've got her ankles free. Now I toss her clothes across the bed to Vadney.

"Jessica," he says just above a whisper. "Think you're strong enough to dress yourself?"

"I think so. My left arm's a little numb. Give me a few minutes to get the circulation back."

He nods. "We'll wait outside. Take all the time—"

"No. Don't go. Just give me a few minutes, I'll be okay."

I hand Vadney the boots, he puts them on the floor, walks around to my side of the bed, escorts me to a spot over near the door. Jessica turns away from us, slides her legs off the bed, sits up, rubs her wrists. Her shadow is large on the far wall and window shade as she gets dressed slowly and laboriously.

Finally, when she tries to stand, she can't quite make it. Chief and I go over quickly, each take an elbow, help her up, walk her slowly to the door.

"How long have I been here?" she asks.

"We don't know for sure," I tell her. "Day and a half, somewhere in there."

"What's today?"

"Thursday night, October twentieth."

"What time is it?"

Glance at my watch. "Eight fifty-five."

"Seems like I've been here at least two or three days. Feels like it, anyway."

Open the door, go out in the hall, Brendan takes one look at Jessica, his eyes say it all. His eyes say how I feel. Deep inside. I glance back at the room. Light from the unseen bathroom to the left throws a pale yellow rectangle across the worn carpet and the rectangle bends upward and slants across the dirty single sheet on the bed. What happened in this room? What did this sick animal do to her? How bad will the after-shocks be? How long will it take her to return to normal, if she ever does?

How long have I been here?

What's today?

What time is it?

Jim Mairs rushes Jessica off to Bellevue for a comprehensive physical, Chief speeds Jerry Grady, Brendan, and me to the Sixtieth Precinct, 2951 West Eighth Street, Brooklyn. Funny feeling walking into this modern precinct now, I worked out of the old Sixtieth as a rookie back in 1955, shield number 23200. Lucked into the double ciphers, pure chance; add up the numbers, you get a lucky seven. Back then, it was a beautiful old station house, looked much the same as the Nineteenth does today. Stone stoop out front, big arched entrance, heavy double doors, wooden staircase going up to the squadroom, brass rail in front of the high desk, switchboard to the right. To the left was another switchboard, they had two in that house. For the simple reason, one covered your call-boxes, because there were so many foot-patrolmen calling in during the summer months, so they had one covering that and the other covering outside calls.

Had a lot of fun in that old house. One story comes to mind, I was working the boardwalk with a partner, can't remember the kid's name now, midsummer day, usual big crowds. See, in the summertime, the Coney Island boardwalk was always full of cops, you needed all you could get. So, what happened, here's this big black guy, huge, about Brendan's size, six-six, maybe 260, 270, built like Sonny Liston, and he's been drinking heavily. So, we're observing him, he's wandering around, now he goes over and sexually abuses a lady who's pushing a baby carriage. What he does, actually, he grabs her ass, she screams bloody murder. We run over there, we step in, he's still grabbing her, we try to arrest him. He resists, of course, he's bombed out of his skull, he decides he wants to fight. We start hitting him with our sticks, it's like hitting a refrigerator. Meantime, he's landing some pretty good punches. Now we're joined by eight other cops, *eight,* all swinging. Slam this monster in the head, across the kneecaps, he's bleeding all over the place, he won't go down, can't get the cuffs on him. Keeps ducking and punching us off like we're dwarfs, we're going up and down like ten Yo-Yos. Finally, a mounted cop gallops up, they were all over the boardwalk in the summer, he charges over, maneuvers around, manages to knock the big guy down with the rear end of his horse. We jump on the sucker, get the cuffs on him, that's that. Takes eleven cops and a horse to drop this geek.

Proud old Sixtieth Precinct was torn down in the late 1960s. Hated to see it go, but change is the price of progress. Or so I'm told. Precinct here now is exactly like all the other new ones around the city, sleek, modern, cost-efficient, without a trace of character or tradition. Walk in here, you think you're in a new city hospital: Sparkling-clean terrazzo floors, pale-blue terra-cotta walls, off-white acoustical ceilings, hidden but bright fluorescent lights, color-coordinated furniture. New

Sixtieth was one of the first precincts to experiment with the height of the front desk. Team of high-priced psychologists came up with the idea that the high desk was unnecessarily intimidating and adversarial to the citizenry, so they recommended a normal-height desk in the belief that the desk officer would have a better basic *rapport* with said citizens. Interesting experiment. Total disaster. Only thing the good psychologists didn't take into consideration was the fact that the overwhelming majority of citizens who're booked at this friendly desk happen to be your standard New York career criminals, an increasing percentage of whom, today, are dopers and head-cases to begin with, space cadets who aren't particularly sensitive to the dynamic psychodrama of police-public rapport. Soon as the normal-height desk was installed here, it was apparent that a potential problem was posed by the physical accessibility of the desk officer to the citizen. During the first year of the experiment, the good psychologists were appraised of the fact that exactly 162 citizens actually attempted to assault the desk officer. Yeah. Relatively small percentage, but significant if you happened to be the officer who wound up spitting teeth. Experiment was discontinued. Team of psychologists submitted a formal report concluding that "the proximity factor proved counterproductive to administrative efficiency." Must be fun to be an egghead. Wonder how much that study cost.

Back to reality as we know it. Marty Shugrue and Dave Pearson escort Laslo from his holding cell to Commander Bill Boggs's office, sit him in the corner away from the window, keep the cuffs on because he'll be transported to the Nineteenth Precinct forthwith, where a line-up will be conducted tonight.

Boggs comes around his desk, big muscular guy, balding, young for a commander, late thirties, sharp as they come. "Mr. Laslo," he says quietly, walking over to him. "I'm going to tell you this just one more time for the record. You have the right to be represented by an attorney of your choice. If you can't afford—"

"All right, let's cut the *crap!*" Laslo snaps. "Let's cut the *posturing* for Vadney's benefit. Get some scumbag from Legal Aid to cover your asses. I don't give a fuck who you get."

"Marty," Chief says, "get Arnold Grossman on the phone, get him at home, explain the situation, ask him to get up to Nineteen as soon as possible with somebody from Legal Aid. Dave, contact all the witnesses, even the reluctant, tell 'em we got our man, arrange transportation to Nineteen immediately, no exceptions. Jerry, get on the horn, alert the media, everybody you can get, tell 'em we hit the jackpot, get 'em to Nineteen pronto." Glances at his watch. "Nine twenty-five now, tell 'em our ETA is ten, that'll get 'em hoppin'. Little John, call the Nineteenth squadroom, get a lineup organized, starting time ten-thirty. We need six heads, six good-looking heads dressed like this slime here. Brendan, call the Twentieth, find out what we confiscated from Laslo's room at that West Side apartment. If there's any jewelry, have 'em rush it over to Nineteen so the witnesses can get a look, maybe claim some of it. We're gonna wrap this thing tonight."

Rubber to road at 9:45, lead-car escort driven by Rizzutti, shotgunned by Nunzio, Shugrue and Pearson in back, flashing lights, screaming siren. Brendan drives Vadney's car, portable lights aglitter, siren atwitter, Grady up front, Laslo in back between the Duke and me, still awesome in our Darth Vader outfits. Bay Parkway past Eighty-sixth and Ridge and Sixty-fifth and Dahill, north on Ocean, northwest on Prospect, straight on the Gowanus, hang a right into the Brooklyn-Queens Expressway to avoid the tunnel, north to the graceful lighted spans of the Brooklyn Bridge, ninety-nine years young now, gala centennial planned for next summer. Across we go in heavy traffic, downtown Manhattan skyline ablaze to our left, World Trade Center's double towers dwarfing all the rest. Here I am, fifty years old, native New Yorker, street kid from the lower East Side, I'm sitting forward now, I'm taking in this magnificent skyline like a first-time tourist from Boise. Love this city, always have, always will, can't get enough of it, most exciting place in the world, what can I tell you? Exactly 6,775 feet later (including the access ramps, in case you ever get that question in Trivial Pursuits), we're doubling back to get on the Elevated Highway heading northeast, then around the horn at East River Park and due north up FDR Drive, snaking through traffic all the way.

Arrive 10:27, it's carnival time already, Sixty-seventh Street is blocked by barricades from Third to Lexington, whole area is jammed with media trucks, vans, cars, TV crews all over, *paparazzi* climbing the poles. Too late for a sellout crowd, but the night people are here in force, and six mounted cops from the elete Central Park Precinct are on hand anyway, big stallions dropping predictable pellets of farm-fresh fragrance. I take out a cigar, bite off the end, spit it on the floor, light up with a smile. Ready for the show.

Blackface comedy, that is.

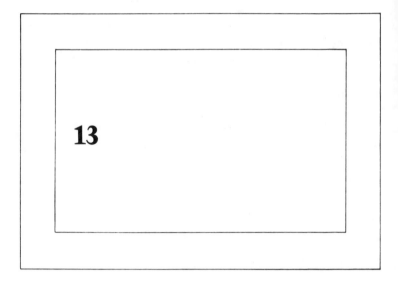

13

TALK ABOUT a made-for-TV spectacle? Mounted cops clear a narrow path through a floodlighted jungle of gawkers, hands on our windows, bodies shoved against our fenders and doors, some *paparazzi* clown even jumps on the hood and starts shooting through the windshield—*flash-click-whine!*—Brendan's temporarily blinded, Grady has to grab the wheel. Pull up at the curb, lights and sirens, all TV cameras rolling, Chief opens the door, yanks Laslo out into an explosion of simultaneous flashes, then a deafening roar when the night people get a load of the Duke's Captain Midnight getup. Veteran newsmen stand aghast; veteran newswomen stand orgasmic. Veteran uniformed cops stand smiling, shoulder-to-shoulder now, both sides of a clearing from the car all the way across the sidewalk and up the stoop to the front door. Chief pauses momentarily on the sidewalk, towering over his cowering captive, strobes flashing like fast disco beats, finally gives 'em a quick, sparkling white, left-sided molar-shower, his sense of drama right on the money, as usual. Escorts Laslo up the old stone steps now, benignly indifferent to the chorus of passionate pleas from all sides—*"Chief, Chief, this way, just one more!"*—because, as they all know only too well, this is merely stage one, the Photo Opportunity stage, in his carefully orchestrated Psychology of Effective Press Relations, to wit: Maximum utilization of time and space within given parameters of minimum lead times necessary for meeting deadlines in both broadcast and print journalism. His formal press conference is scheduled for eleven tonight, immediately following the lineup, and his sense of timing is perfect, of course. Eleven o'clock local news programs will undoubtedly make this their live lead story, billboarding it early for all it's worth. Also, by that time, Jerry Grady will have a fast-and-dirty hard-news press release all typed up neat and clean, the usual 100 Xerox copies three-hole punched and handed out in those distinctive NYPD-blue Duo-Tang 5-3558 presentation folders, ready for the rewrite desk and front-page space in the morning papers. I ask you, does this department have its shit together? Do we give the illusion we're still in control?

Brendan, Jerry, and I get out now, walk behind Marty and Dave as they maneuver their way up the steps past the boys and girls of the media, who're politely discouraged from entering until the press conference. We show our gold to the young uniformed officers at the door, file past the desk, turn left, climb the rickety old steel-reinforced wooden staircase up to the squadroom on the second floor. Controlled bedlam in there, full crew of four-to-midnight-shift detectives doing paperwork, answering phones, interviewing complainants. Laslo's sitting on the floor of the holding cage along with two young space cadets and an older gentleman wino who's sleeping it off, flat on his back, snoring peacefully, already having pissed his knickers (there's no toilet in there), investing the squadroom with a not-unfamiliar late-evening fragrance that, depending on the wino, can be more penetrating than, shall we say, night-blooming jasmine on a breezy summer's eve. Sorry to stick in gritty details like this, but you want the truth, right? I mean, this job ain't all wine and roses, okay?

Chief's in the lieutenant's office talking with ADA Arnold Grossman and the Legal Aid attorney, Anne Meyer. Anne, we've known her for years, she's a joy to watch, probably the finest spitfire Legal Aid ever had. Super-bright diminutive blonde, mid-forties, tortoise-shell glasses, dark ultrafeminine designer outfit. Hails from Georgia originally, speaks with a soft and pleasant drawl, usually a trace of laughter in her voice, but when she's on the warpath, stand back, this kid grabs a meathook, this little lady shoots sparks. Reminds me of Doris Banks. So y'all'll understand, Anne Meyer just ain't about to take no chutzpa from no schmuck, no way, no time, no place, y'honor, suh.

Brendan checks with the property clerk upstairs, shows us the contents of a small suitcase taken from the apartment on 106th Street and rushed over by a detective from the Twentieth Precinct: One Smith & Wesson .38 Combat Masterpiece with a four-inch barrel; one Beretta .22 automatic with a 3.5-inch barrel; one handkerchief containing several dozen pieces of jewelry, including a diamond engagement ring, at least three carats, probably belonging to Belinda Ballanger.

My assignment's relatively easy, rounding up heads to stand in the lineup with Laslo. Usually, I hit the streets, but there's not enough time for that. Lineups in general are a pain in the ass, you lock up some skell on a street surgery charge, now you have to go out with a handful of twenty-dollar-bills and buy his peers to stand in the lineup with him. They all want the money, but want guarantees that nobody can pick them out for something else—not that they did anything wrong lately. Anyway, Chief wants six heads (we only need five, but one acts as an alternate), so I select the best-looking detectives on the four-to-midnight shift: Roger Stephenson, Nuzhat Idrissi, David Perry, Gary Swartzman, J.P. Faber, and Rick Eyerdam, none of whom have ever been seen by any of the witnesses.

By 10:45, Dave Pearson's managed to get eight witnesses transported from their homes to the precinct; they're now in the waiting room downstairs. Only two are missing: Belinda Ballanger, who's still in the private psychiatric institution in Westchester County, and one of the Bronx witnesses who's out of town.

Laslo's taken out of the cage, Anne Meyer has a private conversation with him in the lieutenant's office. Next, Meyer wants to see the six detectives who'll be in the lineup. Meanwhile, ADA Grossman wants to brief the eight witnesses. I accompany him downstairs.

Room is full of women—Dawn Harkness, Sheila McKenzie, Barbara Altman, Gale Jennings, Laura Warren, Cathy Giroux, Susan Antolini—but one really stands out in more ways than one. Looks like a young Sophia Loren in a low-cut black dress with two beauties that won't quit. Grossman catches me staring.

"Who is she?" I whisper.

"Angela Petrocelli."

"No wonder uncle Tito got upset."

Grossman calls the girls to order, gives them a brief rundown on the basic mechanics of a lineup, explains the legal requirement of a definitive answer: Yes or no, period, no qualifications. Brendan comes in and tells us Meyer's satisfied with the appearance of the lineup men and is ready to proceed.

Primarily because of the convenience factor, most lineups these days are held downtown in the Manhattan DA's office, 155 Leonard, around the corner from the Criminal Courts Building, 100 Centre Street, but most precincts have a small lineup room and ours isn't too bad. Each individual witness stands in a small soundproofed viewing room behind a one-way glass window and looks at "suspects" in the brightly lighted lineup room. Only three other people are permitted in the viewing room with the witness: An assistant DA, the suspect's attorney, and the arresting officer. In the lineup room, the suspect stands against a wall with five others and each wears a large white card around his neck with a black number from one to six. An intercom system allows the ADA, attorney, or arresting officer to speak to any of the suspects, addressing each by number, asking questions, telling them to move, and so on. Before the next witness enters the viewing room, the suspects are required to exchange numbers.

It's now 10:55, we're almost a half hour behind schedule, so we hustle the ladies down to the basement lineup room pronto. Suspects are already inside, Chief's standing by the door of the viewing room, frowning, looking at his watch. He's washed the black grease paint from his puss and changed from his dashing jumpsuit, but his jacket, tie, and shoes are still in the ESD van, wherever that is, along with Brendan's and mine. Somehow, Duke Wayne in sneakers doesn't make it.

First witness to go in is Dawn Harkness, because her mother's waiting for her upstairs. Grossman escorts her in, followed by Meyer and Vadney. Door closes. Now the other girls sit nervously, some smoking, all eyeing each other.

Brendan and I go upstairs to the big bathroom off the locker area, climb out of our jumpsuits, laborously scrub off the grease paint. Now we go up to the squadroom, looking for Jim Mairs. There he is in Big John Daniel's office, on the phone, all our jackets, ties, and shoes arranged neatly on the table nearby. How he orchestrates all this shit is beyond me. Tell you what, I'm so glad to get out of these turned-up sneakers I could scream for joy. We grab Vadney's gear, head downstairs. When we make the turn on the ground floor, we see the boys and girls of the media still outside waiting impatiently. It's 11:10, the local TV news shows are well underway, but there's still plenty of time to break in live. In fact, it's much more dramatic that way.

Outside the lineup room, Marty Shugrue gives us a happy update. One by one the victims picked out Laslo and signed statements to that effect. Dave Pearson tells us that almost all the jewelry has now been identified by the victims; only exceptions are the diamond engagement ring and two bracelets, probably all belonging to Belinda Ballanger. He's called Mr. Ballanger and asked him to identify the pieces tomorrow morning in the property clerk's office at headquarters.

Angela Petrocelli is in the viewing room now, last one, and she's taking her time. When she comes out at 11:15, she looks very disturbed, leaves immediately. Turns out she refused to identify him. When Grossman asks her if she sees the man who raped her, she just stares at Laslo, nods, says, "Yes." He asks her what number the man's wearing. She says, "That doesn't matter. I told the detective I'd look at the lineup and I have. Now, if you don't mind, I'd like to leave."

And away she goes. My opinion, this more or less verifies the word on the street that Tito Petrocelli was seriously attempting to get a positive ID. Angela, probably against her will, was sent here to identify him first-hand, just to be absolutely certain we have the right man. Knowing Tito, he's not the type guy to put out a contract on hearsay; too expensive. Confirms my suspicion that Laslo may be harder to keep alive than we think.

Lineup's over, seven out of eight statements signed and sealed, Laslo's taken upstairs to the holding cage. Chief's ready to meet the media now. Smiles when he sees we've got his best blue blazer, tie, and shoes. Goes in the lineup room, ties his tie carefully in front of the window that's a mirror from that side, puts on his shoes and blazer, gives orders as he carefully combs his hair:

"Brendan, call Grady in the squadroom, tell him to go down and pass out the press release. I'll give a five-minute conference on the front steps—repeat, on the front steps—at eleven-twenty sharp."

Brendan gets on the phone.

Chief inspects his pearly whites in the mirror. "Marty, where you got the two lessies?"

"Lieutenant's office."

"Go up, escort 'em down, get 'em in the lead car." Adjusts his tie, glances at Pearson in the mirror. "Dave, got the motorcycle escort all set?"

"Yes, sir, ready to go."

"Four of 'em?"

"Yes, sir. Two front, two rear."

Turns to me now. "Little John, you and Brendan go get Laslo, cuff him, bring him down, wait by the front desk till I finish the conference. Now, listen up, buddy. On my cue line, 'Arraignment is scheduled for midnight tonight,' you guys hustle him down the steps—the three of us surround him, y'know—and into my car, the second car there. Brendan drives, you and me in back with Laslo, Anne and Arnold in front."

"You got it."

Checks his general appearance one last time. "All right, let's go to work."

Off to work we go. Chief orchestrates the five-minute press conference with the panache of Ed Koch and the *cajónes* of Ron Reagan. There he goes again. While he's fielding final questions in the blinding dazzle of TV lights and flashing strobes, Brendan and I wait inside near the front desk with Laslo, cuffed, backed up by Meyer and Grossman. Shugrue and Pearson are already in the lead car with Gale Jennings and Laura Warren. Grossman has telephoned the Westchester County District Attorney, it's been agreed to prosecute the rape and robbery charges here first, then turn Laslo over to them for the murder charge. Although Laslo's been booked on four counts of robbery in the first and eight counts of rape in the first, Grossman has decided to actually prosecute on just one case, Jennings and Warren, the two lesbians; they're excellent witnesses and it's the only case where we have corroboration, a critical factor in the successful prosecution of rape cases. However, he feels the case may never get to trial. Meyer has already indicated that, during the arraignment, she'll request immediate and comprehensive psychiatric testing at Bellevue. When we discuss the Petrocelli situation with Grossman, he tells us he'll suggest to the judge that Rikers' isolation wing would be safer than Bellevue.

On Vadney's loud and clear cue line, "Arraignment is scheduled for midnight tonight," the four of us surround Laslo, hustle him down the steps in the merciless glare of celebrity and into the second of the two waiting cars. Chief jumps in next to Laslo and me; Brendan, Anne, and Arnold squeeze in front; all doors are slammed, and our motorcycle escort takes off with full sirens in the space already cleared by our Royal Mounties. TV cameras whir, motor-drives whine, reporters gasp, night people roar. One of the few times in my career I've ever been on TV. Couldn't be helped. Wonder if Catherine's watching. How sweet it is!

Within a few minutes we're on FDR Drive heading south. Turned out to be a pleasant autumn night after all, reflections dancing on the East River, almost makes you forget all the dirt. Reach the back entrance of the recently renovated Tombs on Baxter Street. From here on, it's all routine. Laslo's photographed, given a "B" number, printed again, placed in the holding pen directly behind the arraignment room, or 1B, as we call it. We join Marty and Dave in the complaint room with Jennings and Warren, sign the documents, go back for Laslo, take him into 1B. Here we're met by Grossman, Meyer, and the judge, Richard N. Roffman. Bail is refused. Meyer requests Bellevue, Grossman insists on Rikers' isolation wing. Laslo's remanded to Rikers.

Early edition of the *News* has a hilariously unflattering front-page photo of Vadney in blackface escorting Laslo up the front steps of the Nineteenth, obviously selected by a giggling Vinnie Casandra. Big bold headline:

BRONX COP NABBED
IN RAPE-ROBBERY-
MURDER RAMPAGE

Friday, October 21, 10:05 A.M., we're in the squadroom starting to catch up on paperwork when we get a call from Vadney:
"Laslo's in Elmhurst General Hospital, attempted suicide last
night. Tied his prison shirt to the cell bars at Rikers, tried to
hang himself, nearly made it. Now the doctors fear possible
brain damage."

Turns out there's no brain damage. Grossman and Meyer
speak with Judge Roffman, arrangements are made to transfer
him tonight to the new wing of Kings County Hospital in
Brooklyn. Security is excellent there and it's more convenient
for psychiatric testing because our doctors have their offices
in that building.

Monday, October 24, 4:10 P.M. We're about to call it a day
when the chief calls, angry as hell: Laslo tried it again, this
time his wrists. Correction over there frisks him three times
a day, but it seems someone slipped a razor blade in his food.
They're stitching him up now, but apparently he's lost a considerable amount of blood. Chief orders an immediate full-
scale investigation. My opinion, it's a total waste of time. Any
con in that place could've slipped it in his food; Laslo's not the
most popular guy around. Also, for all we know, our pal Tito
might have an open contract out on him, heavy bread up for
grabs, so the guy's not going to be safe anywhere. Now Vadney gets in touch with the Commissioner of Corrections, demands that Laslo be placed in a padded cell and spoon-fed if
necessary. Says, "The people of the City of New York want
and deserve the truth in an open trial by jury and, by Christ,
they're gonna get it! Put the fucker in a straitjacket where he
belongs!"

Tuesday, October 25, 11:15 A.M. Grossman receives two reports from the State psychiatrists indicating that Laslo is competent to stand trial. He hasn't heard from the defense but was
informed that a top private psychiatrist named Dr. Barry E.
Mukamal had seen Laslo twice. However, Grossman's spoken

with his bureau chief and it looks very much like it won't go to trial. He expects Anne Meyer to request a plea-bargaining meeting, provided Laslo is not found to be mentally incompetent. Should they go to trial, State will look for the max twenty-five to life. On a plea-bargain, they'd consider fifteen to twenty, which doesn't mean squat anyway because his butt is cooked in Yonkers. Grossman's now awaiting Dr. Mukamal's psychiatric report.

Gets it about 1:15 that afternoon. Meeting is scheduled for 3:30 in Judge Roffman's chambers. Present are the two State shrinks, Dr. Mukamal, Meyer, Grossman. Dr. Mukamal has administered an extremely comprehensive psychiatric examination, including a CAT scan and a series of blood and skin tests. He's established beyond a reasonable doubt that Laslo was born with a chromosomal aberration, to wit: the famed "extra Y" chromosome (XYY), a genetic defect discovered in extensive scientific studies to be a common denominator among convicted criminals who exhibit violent antisocial behavior. Dr. Mukamal concludes that from the moment the dormant condition was triggered on September 13, 1983, Laslo was not capable of controlling his emotions, physically or mentally, and therefore is not competent to stand trial. State shrinks counter that they're thoroughly familiar with the controversial XYY studies, but don't believe there's enough evidence to establish a definite causal relationship between this genetic defect and deviance. Judge Roffman deliberates, finally decides Laslo's mentally competent, sets the trial date for November 30; he will preside.

Meeting breaks up, Grossman and Meyer have a powwow, as expected. Meyer's ready to make a deal. Accepts the plea, fifteen to twenty, to cover all cases in Manhattan and the Bronx. However, she's definitely going to trial in the homicide case. They confer with Judge Roffman, trial date is canceled, sentencing is scheduled for Friday, October 28, 10:30 A.M., State Supreme Court, Part 45.

Chief's briefed on all this, of course, and we get an unexpected reaction. After all his "trial and truth" routine, he's sick of the bad press, sick of the psychological damage to the department, sick of Commissioner Reilly's meddling. Says he's satisfied with the outcome, he'll be happy to have the scumbag completely out of our jurisdiction, sooner the better. Orders Brendan and me to handle the sentencing and delivery to the Yonkers people.

Brendan calls Yonkers PD, relates that Laslo will be available to them after his court appearance on Friday. They confirm they'll have two detectives and two Corrections officers from Sing Sing Prison down on that date. After sentence, Laslo will be taken to Ossining where he'll be remanded pending trial on the Westchester homicide. I call the hospital, bring Corrections there up to date. Laslo will be delivered to the Tombs in a straitjacket, along with all his papers, on Friday, 10:15 A.M.

Friday, October 28, 8:45 A.M. Brendan and I make copies of all our reports for the Yonkers PD, then drive down to Grossman's office on Leonard where we meet the two detectives from Yonkers and the two Corrections officers from Sing Sing. Laslo's delivered to the Tombs slightly ahead of schedule, 10:10. Grossman accompanies the four officers to State Supreme Court on Centre Street, Brendan and I go over to the Tombs. Sure enough, Laslo's in a straitjacket. Looks pale and exhausted. We remove the straitjacket immediately; he's wearing his dark turtleneck sweater and jeans. Now we cuff him, walk him to the courthouse, take the elevator up, have him placed in the holding pen for Part 45, just back of the courtroom.

At 10:25, the courtroom is about half full, mostly press people, undoubtedly disappointed they were denied the opportunity to see what should've been a fascinating trial. Brendan and I take our seats next to the Yonkers detectives and Corrections officers. One of the officers opens a small bag, removes a pair of leg-irons; we never use them, but they have their own rules.

All rise as Judge Roffman enters promptly at 10:30. Court officer hands him a copy of the calendar for the day. He summons Grossman and Meyer to the bench. After a brief conversation, they return to their seats. Now the court officer calls Docket 2219 for sentencing: Ronald Drake Laslo, charged with rape and robbery, first degree. Brendan and I walk quickly out the side door and back to the holding pen, escort Laslo into the courtroom, stand him next to Meyer, then stand on either side of them at the table.

Judge Roffman puts on his glasses, clears his throat, reads from the affidavit: "Do you, Ronald Drake Laslo, plead guilty to the charges of rape and robbery in the first degree, in that on the day—"

BLAM! BLAM! Laslo falls forward, face down on the table, courtroom explodes with shouts and screams, almost everybody hits the floor fast. I whirl around in a crouch, shaking, see one of the uniformed court officers leap the rail and pounce on somebody in the front row; another officer jumps the rail right behind him. There's so much confusion, I can't even see who they've got. Laslo's been hit in the head and upper back, blood's splattered all over the table. Now I look around, the two court officers have a woman in custody, dressed in black with a black hat and veil. Judge shouts above the noise, tells the court stenographer to call an ambulance from Beekman Downtown Hospital, which is only a few blocks away, orders the courtroom cleared, then tells the officers to bring the woman into his chambers immediately. Laslo's still face down on the table and not moving. He looks dead. Brendan and I follow Grossman and Meyer into the judge's chambers.

When we get inside, the woman is seated in a chair, head down, face in her hands, sobbing. Grossman kneels down, tries to get a look at her face behind her hands and black veil.

"What's your name?" he asks quietly.

She keeps her head down, doesn't answer. She has the legal right to do that, of course, we can't force her to say anything.

"Will you please remove your veil?" Grossman asks.

She doesn't answer, doesn't move.

"Who's got the gun?" I ask.

One of the court officers hands me the weapon. Says she was still pointing it when he grabbed it from her. It's a Smith & Wesson .38 Chief's Special, Model 36, same as my own.

"What's your name?" Brendan asks quietly.

No response.

He begins reading her her rights very softly. Seems strange, not even knowing who she is, but that's the way the system works.

Then I notice she doesn't have a purse. I hurry out into the courtroom just in time to see one of our better-dressed Bowery bums walking toward the doors with a black umbrella and purse tucked under his arm. They frequent the courts down here, you can't really keep them out. I break into a run, catch up to him at the door, grab his arm, turn him around.

"What you got there, friend?"

"Got, sir?" Looks at me indignantly, then touches the purse and umbrella. "Oh, these, sir. I was just about to look for the owner."

"I know the owner." I show my gold, grab the purse and umbrella, then take a long look at his eyes, decide he's not worth the time to collar. I turn, walk back down the aisle.

"In God we trust," he calls after me. "Isn't that what it says, sir?"

As I walk, I open the purse, remove a small black wallet, flip it open. There's a plastic holder containing about a dozen credit cards. Name on the first card makes me stop in my tracks. I feel like I've been punched in the stomach.

Two paramedics have just arrived, one black, one white. A small crowd surrounds them as they examine Laslo on the table. I can see his face now. The bullet that entered the back of his head made an exit the size of a quarter in his forehead. The other exited through his larynx. He looks dead, but I've seen worse cases who survived.

"Is he alive?" I ask the paramedics.

Black guy glances at me, shakes his head negatively.

Walk back to the judge's chambers, take Grossman and Brendan aside, open the wallet, show them the card. Their faces say it all.

Now I go over, kneel down beside this lovely girl who's still crying quietly, almost silently, head down. The black veil is wet now and clings to her face. I'm moved to tears, I can't help it. I wait, then speak very softly.

"I understand, Jessica. We all do."

About the Author

John Minahan is the author of fourteen books,
including the Doubleday Award-winning novel
A Sudden Silence, the million-copy best seller
Jeremy, and the first two thrillers in this series,
The Great Hotel Robbery and *The Great
Diamond Robbery.* An alumnus of Cornell,
Harvard, and Columbia, he is a former staff
writer for *Time* magazine and was editor and
publisher of *American Way* magazine. Minahan
and his wife, Verity, live in Miami.